His kiss foretold
the pleasure to come

He towered over her, his eyes dark, glittering slits in the moonlight.

"Dawn," he murmured against her mouth. His breath seared her everywhere it touched, and she did not understand the wild response that exploded within her. She could feel nothing but Byron's presence, his hands upon her, and her need of him.

He whispered, "Dawn, love...let's go inside—together."

And then she remembered Hilary. He had come from Hilary to her. He had manipulated her with his expert sensuality and made her forget her purpose here, her dislike of him... using her for his own needs, without thought or care for her own.

Using her as a balm to his ego—after a fight with his fiancée!

REBECCA FLANDERS

falkone's promise

Harlequin Books

TORONTO • NEW YORK • LONDON
AMSTERDAM • PARIS • SYDNEY • HAMBURG
STOCKHOLM • ATHENS • TOKYO • MILAN

Harlequin Presents first edition February 1984
ISBN 0-373-10666-1

Original hardcover edition published in 1983
by Mills & Boon Limited

CHAPTER ONE

THERE was an enchantment to the land, one which Dawn had read about in the dozens of travel brochures she had accumulated and dreamed about every night for the past two weeks, but nothing had prepared her for the very real majesty and mystery of the Scottish Hebrides. She had felt it from the moment she had stepped off the commuter plane at the tiny, old-fashioned airport at Oban. It was in the fresh, damp air that blew across her face through the open window as the little car now wound its way up the north coast. But never had it been so striking as when she had caught her first glimpse of Falkone's Acres.

Its gothic peaks and towers rose tantalisingly from the wooded island as she boarded the ferry that was to take her across, and she found herself straining for more as each creeping sea mile was put behind them, eagerness and anticipation swelling to a flutter in her heart and a tightness in her throat. The ancient castle faded with a mist and grew close again, dipped behind the covering of trees and reappeared, and with each reappearance it became more alluring, like a flirtatious woman withholding promises.

Dawn Morrison had been waiting over three years for an assignment like this. When she had taken the job as an assistant photo-journalist on the staff of a widely read travel magazine she had expected her life to be filled with adventure and glamour. Until now, the farthest she had been from New York was the Grand Canyon—and that was on vacation. When she heard the assignment on Falkone's Acres was coming up she had fought for it, schemed for it, and at last begged for it— and now that she was here, she could hardly believe it.

To her disappointment, nothing could be seen of the actual castle as they docked. In fact, the scene before her was the perfect antithesis of the gothic romance she had imagined it would be. Signs of busy industrialisation were everywhere. Cranes lifted large cases on to waiting barges, and from the watchtower someone with a megaphone barked unintelligible instructions to the dozens of workers who kept their own easy pace on the ground below. Several other cars got off the ferry with the car that carried Dawn and proceeded to take one of the asphalt roads that branched out in several directions. Dawn knew that Falkone's Acres was far better known for its modern-day distillery than its historic past, and that progress was the order of the day, but it was still rather disillusioning to come face-to-face with that fact so soon.

The driver turned off the main road, leaving the bustle behind them, and here the scenery became more interesting. On either side were neat little whitewashed cottages which Jeff, her taciturn and craggy driver, explained were rented by the distillery workers. Housewives beat rugs over their back fences or hung laundry on lines strung between trees, and occasionally a sheep grazed placidly on a front lawn. Then the cottages were left behind and gave way to fields of rolling grain, orchards and meadowland.

'Is it very far to the castle?' she asked suddenly.

'Not more'n a mile,' he replied, not glancing at her as he spat a stream of brown tobacco juice out the window.

'Then—I know this might sound silly—but I'd like to walk the rest of the way. To get some shots, you know.'

He slowed the car to a stop. 'No business o' mine. Stay direct to the road,' he added as she got out, dragging her camera bag with her, 'an' ye can't miss it.'

She waved cheerfully and received not a backward glance as he drove away.

She had more than one reason for wanting to walk, but immediately the little car disappeared from sight she wondered if she had done the right thing. As with all new situations, she felt a little ill at ease and she had thought the walk might give her a chance to gain her composure and allow her to give the impression of intense professional dedication she most of all wanted to project. She did most earnestly want to make a good impression on these people, the wealthy aristocracy of a foreign culture, but now she wondered if her decision to walk might be deemed too independent, or a flaunting of their hospitality, or a display of eccentricity.

It was true that when one accepted an assignment or contracted for the completion of a task one was representing the company and must keep that in mind at all times. What did not seem fair was that when an American went abroad she seemed to be held responsible for the reputation of the entire nation, and in Dawn's case, in whatever she did she felt herself to be representing females everywhere. She did not want to appear to be one of those brash, aggressive American women she had heard Europeans so loved to mock, but she would have to go a long way towards curbing her natural impulses to maintain a low profile.

Her editor often teased her about having an inferiority complex, an accusation which immediately made her well-known temper flare. In actual fact, it was probably closer to the truth than she would ever admit. There was nothing inferior about her work, nor a fear of it, for she was good at what she did and she knew it. But there was a great deal of resentment because she had to work twice as hard as anyone else to prove it. Like a person with a handicap, she was constantly pushing herself to excellence to prove herself as good as anyone else, and Dawn's handicap was her own striking good looks.

She had an ethereal, fairy-like beauty, which she tried to disguise with sternly tailored suits in heavy fabrics and harsh lines. Rarely, even on the most lighthearted social occasions, were her slender shoulders bared or the svelte lines of her body revealed through shimmery crêpes or jerseys. She had a diminutive, doll-like face, deceptively innocent, accented by large, misty-grey eyes. But her most arresting feature was her hair. A peculiar blend of mink and flax, it needed no artificial bleaching or streaking to bring out the summery highlights of a thousand shades of blonde and brown, and it cascaded in a shimmery fall of silk down her back. This, too, she disguised by wearing it tightly braided or knotted and pinned up on her head, for her feminine characteristics, she had discovered, were her worst enemy in the fight for success in the business world.

She wished now she had behaved properly and arrived on the castle grounds in the car sent for her, rather than to come tramping through the woods like a vagrant. She was to be the guest of these people, Margaret and Byron Boyd, for two weeks while completing her assignment, and it was very important to get off on the right foot. Like most artists, she was invariably influenced by her environment, and it would be very difficult to produce a sensitive piece in an atmosphere of hostility and disapproval.

At the moment it was very hard to imagine such an atmosphere could exist, however, as the scenery around her became more and more absorbing. The countryside bore a visage of almost studied neglect, nature run rampant in trailing vines and twisted trees, black rocks jutting here and there randomly. The scent of wild heather permeated the air, and when she wandered a little off the road she discovered the most astounding thing—a perfect circle of sea thrift, about six feet in diameter, growing wild in the woods. She had seen the bright pink plant climbing the cliffs as they approached from the sea, noticed it brightening the shoreline of other islands along the way, but had not imagined it could grow so far away from the ocean. With an exclamation of delight, she snapped several shots and mentally filed it away as a good topic for dinner-table conversation tonight with her host and hostess. It was then that she first noticed the strange sound.

Perhaps it had been there all along, such a low, monotonous note that it hardly claimed notice over the joyful chirping of the birds—repetitive chords now joined by a soft strumming in a higher key, and she recognised a guitar.

Had curiosity not prompted her to follow, professional pride would have. This was one shot she simply must have—lowly shepherd boy and guitar reposing in the glen, dreaming love songs on a lazy spring morning.

In her sensible tweed pants suit and sturdy travelling shoes she did not hesitate about clambering to the top of a rocky mound near the side of the road for a better view. And there, squatting down low, she caught her breath, for he was much closer than she had thought. Directly below her and only a few yards away, leaning against the tree whose branches she had to duck her head to avoid, was not a boy at all, but a full grown man. His head was bent in profile away from her over a guitar and his fingers lightly brushed the random chords in a sad, almost eerie melody.

She studied him with a artist's eye, both intrigued and a little awed by the picture he presented. He was wearing tight jeans and black turtleneck sweater, the muscles of his thighs and arms were taut and sinewy, clearly outlined as they strained against the material. The chest which cradled the guitar was broad and his hands were large, long slender fingers wielding a peculiar fascination in the rhythmic stroking motions they made against the strings of the instrument. His hair was jet black and rather long, and his eyelids were heavily fringed with long, dark lashes. His face, too, was dark, in the manner of the Scots, shadowed by the branches of the tree and the hint of a beard. His expression as he bent over the instrument might have been great sorrow or thinly reined violence, his lips were tightly compressed and his facial muscles taut. It was a black mood, and he definitely gave the impression of one who did not wish to be disturbed.

This put her in a very awkward situation. She dared not begin clicking the shutter of her camera, although her fingers itched to do so. Character profiles were her most absorbing hobby, and she could hardly have wished for a better subject than this. Neither had she the courage to break his self-absorption and ask permission, and at any rate that would only shatter the mood. Her only choice was to climb down as quickly and as quietly as she had got up, and hope that she escaped unnoticed.

Carefully, she inched back, seeking her footing, straightening a little to turn. But as she did so a branch snagged on the single clasp that pinned up her hair, she jerked in surprise and pain, and the ornament went tumbling down the rock to strike him on the shoulder. Her braid swung loose and forward towards him and she simply knelt there on all fours, looking and feeling very foolish.

His first expression as he looked around was surprise, then swift anger, and then a softening which might have been amusement as he spied her among the branches. His eyes, she noticed, were as dark as his hair, and could be very foreboding when reflecting such a rapid assault of emotions as she had just witnessed.

He got slowly to his feet, setting the guitar aside, and came towards her. He was very tall. Directly below her, his hands on his hips, his face tilted towards her, he said softly, 'Rapunzel, Rapunzel, let down your hair . . .' And in his eyes was a light of soft appreciation as his gaze travelled over her face, her small, perfectly shaped body, and the long rope of light hair that almost touched his shoulder.

Dawn was embarrassed, and annoyed for that embarrassment, and her tone was somewhat sharper than it should have been as she replied, 'I'm nothing of the sort, I assure you. I merely heard the music . . .'

There might have been a hardening of his eyes as one brow quirked, but it quickly disappeared as he drawled smoothly, 'A spy, in my carefully-guarded fortress?' His hand reached forward to clasp her braid lightly. 'Shall I climb up to you, Rapunzel-spy, or will you come down?'

She shrank back. 'I'll come down the same way I came up,' she answered stiffly. 'I'm sorry I disturbed you.'

She turned on her toes to do so, and suddenly her uncertain balance gave way. She tottered for a moment, smothering a little shriek of surprise in her throat, and then she felt strong hands clasp her waist. He swung her from the rock and into his arms before she could so much as utter a startled gasp.

Cradling her against his chest like a child, his dark eyes snapping and his lips parted in laughter very close to hers, he said, 'The Irish have their leprechauns, we have our fairy-spies, and it's considered very good luck to catch one.'

Dawn was scarlet with embarrassment. His arms were strong and powerful, he supported her weight with no effort at all and she felt no sign of his easing his grip. His warmth penetrated her at all points where their bodies touched and she could feel the slow, steady beat of his heart against her breast. About him was the faintly alluring scent of masculinity and whisky, and the way his dark eyes raked her in amusement made her wretchedly aware of her undignified position.

She said, struggling for a modicum of composure, 'Please let me go.'

His eyes were lit with a soft sensual gleam as they travelled over her face; her heart leapt and began to pound as she understood the intent in that gleam. He was confident of his power and was thoroughly enjoying the game, she was suddenly much too aware of his closeness, of his straining chest muscles against her breasts, of the band of his arm beneath her hips and of the warmth of his breath on her face. He said softly, 'If I do, will you grant me a wish?'

She stammered stupidly, 'Wh-what?' Something was happening to her in his arms. She was rapidly losing the power of rational thought beneath the numbing onslaught of sensual impressions he seemed to be arousing. Common sense and the instinct for self-preservation were deserting her with every moment he held her.

'I told you,' he said, his eyes magnetising her with that strange light, 'to catch a fairy spy is very good luck . . .' his voice was husky, 'but to kiss one is even better . . .'

And with no further warning, his lips moved to hers, a light brush of electric warmth that explored delicately even as it promised more, and left her for a moment completely helpless to the sudden shock of unexpected sensations that gentle touch generated. For a moment, no more, she was captured in his spell, she felt a rush of rising response to what seemed to her no more than the combined magic of time and place—the tall dark stranger in the mystical wood, the flare of romance, the sudden, electrifying sensation . . . and then, just as she felt his arms tighten about her with the deepening of his kiss and her own response became impossible to hide, quick saving reason returned. She turned her face and pushed violently at his chest, she found her feet somewhat unsteadily on the ground and the next thing she knew she was looking up into a pair of wickedly dancing black eyes.

She was aghast at her own behaviour, embarrassed over the entire situation, and furious because he was laughing at her. She did not know what to say. With flaming cheeks and glittering eyes, she stepped forward to brush past him, but he blocked her way. Pretending not to notice, she started to move around him, but with a slight move of his body he prevented her again. She lifted her eyes angrily and found herself staring straight into his chest.

Being a small person, Dawn was invariably intimidated by those larger than she, and invariably she tried not to show it. Though she was very much aware of her position as 'mouse' in this game of cat-and-mouse he was playing she lifted her eyes defiantly to look squarely into his and demanded, 'Let me pass, please.'

His eyes twinkled. 'And suppose I choose not to?'

Embarrassment, frustration and helplessness combined to make her temper flare as hotly as her cheeks. 'I think you're rude, presumptuous, and——'

'And I think you,' he interrupted mildly, 'are very attractive.'

'And furthermore,' she sputtered angrily, 'I don't care in the least for your—your adolescent come-ons! Now will you *let me pass*?'

'You didn't answer,' he reiterated calmly. 'What will you do if I don't?'

'For one thing,' she assured him with spirit, 'I'll most certainly scream. For another, if you care at all for your face the way it is——'

'Say no more, fair lady,' he declared, his sides fairly shaking with repressed laughter. 'As it happens, I'm *not* in the market to have my face re-done by the claws of a wildcat. Pray, proceed.' He swept her an elaborate bow, his arm gesturing the way ahead.

Dawn stalked past him, feeling somewhat avenged, when she was struck by a terrible thought. She had left her camera bag on top of the rock! For a moment she debated whether to leave it and continue her dignified exit, but the thought of all that expensive equipment lying about in the woods for thieves dissuaded her. She stopped and, shooting him a dark look of warning, crossed before him again to retrieve the bag.

In this she faced a problem, however. This side of the rock offered no foothold, its surface was slippery and its summit above her head. She stood on tiptoe and groped for it, jumped a little and missed, all the while aware of his eyes boring into her back. And then there was the sound of footsteps moving towards her, and he reached easily for the bag and handed it to her politely.

She glared at him, swung the bag over her shoulder, and started once again to walk away. She had not gone a dozen steps, however, before she heard his voice again. 'Miss Morrison.'

She stopped, and slowly turned, a dreadful fear beginning to form in her chest. He was grinning, and holding her gold hair clasp in his outstretched fingers. He said, 'Yours, I believe?'

Very slowly, she closed the distance between them and took the clasp hesitantly. Her throat felt dry as she managed, 'H-how did you know my name?'

'I wasn't expecting any other female American

photographers today.' He swept her another mocking bow. 'Byron Boyd, at your service, madame.'

She said dully, 'Oh, no!' and stared at him. She did not know what she had expected—someone older, more refined, more ... she did not know what. She added, without thinking, and more to herself than to him, 'I guess I blew it.'

His dark brow quirked provocatively. He agreed, 'If that quaint Americanism is meant to refer to your most unco-operative behaviour a moment ago, yes, you did. There's an old Gaelic saying—never rebuke the well-intentioned advances of the man who butters your bread.'

Dawn refused to succumb to the mortification that was threatening to swallow her whole. After all her careful preparations to make a good impression on her host, after all her determination to prove herself competent and efficient in the performance of this assignment, what had been her first move upon setting foot on foreign soil? She had allowed herself to be swept into a ridiculous fantasy of romance and adventure and flung herself into the arms of a stranger—the arms of her host!—like a starry-eyed schoolgirl. Horrible thoughts burning with embarrassment were racing through her head with the memory and she frantically sought a way to regain lost ground and erase the last few moments from history.

Anger was her best defence, and her eyes began to snap as she twisted up her braid and pinned it securely to the top of her head. She said coolly, 'I can only hope, Mr Boyd, that yours is not an example of Gaelic hospitality. And I think we'd best understand now that I'm here in a *professional* capacity, not for your entertainment, and I don't appreciate one bit being pounced upon in the woods like a—like a——'

'Like a beautiful woman?' he suggested mildly.

She stared him down. 'The fact that I'm a woman,' she responded evenly, 'beautiful or not, shouldn't concern you in the least.'

'Ah, but it does,' he said softly, and his eyes swept over her in a deliberately appreciative manner. 'And please don't try to tell me that you didn't enjoy what happened between us a moment ago—it's a little too late, I'm afraid, for modest protestations.'

She wilfully subdued a renewed flush that threatened to scorch her cheeks, holding on to her composure with a death-grip. 'I am not in the least interested in—what happened a moment ago,' she replied steadily, 'except, perhaps, to feel a mild sense of insult, and to warn you that I don't intend to allow anything similar to happen again.'

He lifted one dark brow in a sardonically quizzical manner. 'I find that very hard to believe,' he said smoothly. 'A woman as lovely as yourself must be interested in all sorts of things besides business. And, for the record, I didn't intend to insult you, I meant it as a compliment. You must be used to them.'

'I am,' she told him coldly. 'Which is precisely why I find it such a bore. And I promise you, the only thing I *am* interested in on this trip is the job I was sent here to do. So if you'll be so kind as to direct me to the castle . . .'

Something in her icy-cold demeanour must have finally got through to him. He looked at first curious, perhaps a little startled, and then a shield as remote as hers came over his face. For some odd reason that look disappointed her. It was as though he had already forgotten her, dismissed her as unworthy of his notice, and that hurt her.

He said in a smooth, expressionless voice. 'My apologies, then, for having bored you.' He turned to pick up his guitar, and as he did he cast a chilling look over his shoulder. 'Since you were impudent enough to start out on foot, I assume you have no objection to continuing in the same manner?'

She nodded, and he gestured without looking at her towards the right. 'The road is just beyond that fir. Continue straight to the north and the castle is less than half a mile away.'

She said stiffly, 'Thank you,' and with a short, impersonal nod, Byron Boyd pushed his way through the bracken and soon was out of sight.

Dawn was left feeling slightly vindicated, but strangely depressed. She could not afford to offend her host. What in the world had got into her? But then it was he who had made the first offensive move . . . wasn't it?

She found herself strangely fascinated by the man who was Byron Boyd—his moods, his banter, his sharp humour. She had been sorry to see that humour fade beneath the mask of cold politeness. He was a man she would have liked to have known better, but she had just destroyed her only chance at that.

Then she remembered something that should have made her feel better, to either dismiss the incident as the childish game it had been, or to despise him thoroughly for the cad he was. But, in fact, it only made her more depressed as she set her steps doggedly for the castle keep. It was Byron and *Margaret* Boyd.

He was married.

CHAPTER TWO

BY the time Dawn reached the castle she was hot, sticky, and discouraged. She would almost have rather died before admit defeat on the first really big assignment she had ever had, but that was now what she was dangerously close to doing. She imagined a very grim two weeks ahead of her, spent mostly trying to avoid Byron Boyd, and as a result a very dry and possibly even unpublishable article to return to the States with her as an example of how far she could go in the business if given a chance. It was all wretchedly unfair!

The castle was approached through an avenue of towering oaks, set upon a slight rise, and faced by an enormous, dark lake which reflected every detail of the stalwart architecture to perfection in the shimmering sunlight. Dawn had to pause and focus her camera, changing lenses for a scope view, back again for the close-up of the twin lions worked in granite which guarded the walkway, moving ever closer until she was suprised to view through the camera the huge oaken door swing open and a tall, middle-aged lady appear in its place.

'Hello!' she called, lifting her arm in greeting. 'You must be Miss Morrison.'

Dawn let the camera drop to its supporting strap about her neck and went quickly up the stone walkway, mounting the wide, bluntly hewn steps as she replied, 'Yes, I am.' She found it not so

19

difficult as she had anticipated to look fresh and eager to begin work.

'When Jeff told us you'd decided to walk, we began to get a little worried about you. It's not an easy trek—all uphill!'

For some reason, Dawn had been prepared to dislike this brisk, stocky lady with the slightly grey hair, but miserably she began to realise it was impossible. Her smile was open and warm, her manner unpretentious and welcoming, yet Dawn could not help wondering how a man such as Byron, so virile and sensual, could have chosen such a plain woman, obviously many years his senior, for his wife.

She apologised as she reached her, 'I'm sorry to have kept you waiting. I thought it was important to get a closer look at the countryside before I began.'

The woman waved it away. 'Not at all. Byron made it clear you were to have the run of the island while you were here.' She extended her hand with another cheerful smile. 'I'm Margaret Boyd.'

Dawn could not help returning the smile as she clasped her hand. 'And my name is Dawn. I'm very pleased to meet you, Mrs Boyd.'

She laughed a little. 'No, it's Miss, and you can call me Maggie. I never married, to my brother's great disappointment. He's stuck with me for life!'

Through her confusion, Dawn was aware of an odd sense of relief. She stammered, 'I'm sorry, I thought you and . . . I'm afraid I assumed I would be meeting husband and wife——'

Margaret Boyd laughed and linked her arm companionably through Dawn's as she lead the way inside. 'No, indeed. We're bachelor and bachelorette, respectively, which I suppose is rather unusual at our age. But life on an island is rather restrictive. Most native islanders marry late and stay married, which is not an altogether bad arrangement, is it?'

She kept up a continuous stream of chatter as they entered the great hall, and Dawn felt the tingle of excitement seep through her once again as she looked about her. The walls were stone, and she noticed immediately a severe drop of temperature which must have been near ten degrees, along with a faint, musky odour which hinted at dampness and antiquity. As her eyes adjusted to the dimness they fell first on the traditional suit of armour, glinting in a shaft of dusty sunlight through the open door, then the Boyd crest occupying a prominent place on the forward wall. It was a brilliant azure with a silver band across the centre, featuring a single hand pointing upwards with the thumb and two fingers extended. Below it was inscribed the motto in flowing letters: *Confido*.

Maggie, noticing the direction of her gaze, explained, 'It means "I trust". A very safe motto to chose in a day when fealty to the king could mean the difference between life and death, wouldn't you say?'

'It's a splendid motto for any day,' Dawn agreed enthusiastically, already feeling herself being drawn into the character of this place. She would not take the time now to set up her tripod and light meter, but come back later for that all-important shot. She was burning to know more of the history of the family. 'Can you tell me a little about the family?'

Maggie laughed. 'Shall I give you my entire tour-speech, or encapsulate it?'

'Either is fine,' Dawn smiled.

'Allow me to suggest the condensed version.'
They both turned at the sound of the masculine
drawl behind them, and Dawn felt her spirits sink.
Byron Boyd stood there, leaning in the doorway,
the moted sunlight dancing off his dark hair,
shadows casting his face into even more severe
lines than she remembered. 'I'm sure Miss
Morrison is tired from her—er—journey, and
would be better equipped to deal with our
formidable annals after she's rested.'

Maggie said, 'Allow me to present my brother,
Miss Morrison, Byron . . .'

Dawn replied, somewhat weakly, 'We've met.'
But she was stung by the steady mockery in his
eyes, the way his tone twisted when he referred to
her 'journey', and she refused to be intimidated by
his deliberate efforts to remind her of their last
meeting. She drew herself up and continued in a
more businesslike tone, pleasant but very professional. 'You're mistaken, Mr Boyd, I would very
much like to hear the history of your family. That
is my business, after all.'

He inclined his head ever so slightly, as though
conceding to her the slightest of victories, and
strolled forward, his hands in his pockets. In the
most perfect imitation of a tour-master, he recited,
'The first known records of the Boyd clan date
back to the year 1066, when they are reported to
have come to Scotland with William the
Conqueror. The baroncy was received by Robert
de Boyd in 1205, and from that point the clan
branched out in many directions. Thomas Boyd
married Princess Mary, daughter of King James
III, in about 1420. James Boyd set up his fortress
on this island in 1536, where it has withstood

many savage attacks through the centuries and was almost demolished during the time of Cromwell. Reconstruction began in 1720, but many features have remained unchanged. You will notice as you ascend the upper staircase scars in the wood which are reported to have been made by the sabres of the lord of the manor in 1613, in defence of his lady-love.' He looked at her. 'We've always been a jealous breed, and distinctively loyal to our ladies.' Her cheeks were burning, for she knew he was enacting this entire charade only to mock her, but he continued airily, 'Our seed is spread far and wide, reaching at last the fair shores of the New World where Benedict Boyd, in 1636, became the first governor of the Rhode Island Colony.' He lifted an eyebrow towards her in direct challenge, as though to say, 'Enough?' and Dawn picked up on it stiffly.

'Thank you, that was most informative.' She turned deliberately back to Maggie, who was scowling at her brother in a typically sisterly fashion.

'But there's much more ...' he pursued, and Maggie interrupted by linking her arm once more through Dawn's.

'I'm sure Miss Morrison will want to rest now, and then, after a nice cup of tea, I'll take her around.'

'Don't bother, sister dear,' said Byron smoothly, stepping forward to take Dawn's other arm in a ridiculously defiant gesture. 'I'm free for the rest of the day and nothing would give me greater delight than to take the young lady on the grand tour.'

With dignity, Maggie stepped back. 'You may begin, then, by showing her to her room.' She smiled reassuringly at Dawn. 'I'll bring a pot up in a quarter of an hour and we'll have a nice chat, all right?'

Byron dropped her arm as soon as they were out of sight of Maggie, but placed his hand lightly upon her waist as they began an almost immediate descent up a narrow, twisting stone stairway. She could feel the heat of his fingers even through her tweed jacket, the caressing motions they made with the movement of her body, and she thought it must be only imagination that made her so uncomfortable. She said, rather loudly to break the monotonous rattle of their footsteps against the stone, 'Where's the scarred wooden railing?'

He replied softly, his voice echoing like a sensuous whisper off the rounded walls, 'This is not the one. We're in a tower now—the tower where, legend has it, William Boyd seduced the daughter of his bitterest enemy and was such an effective lover that the two clans were united and lived happily ever after.' He paused, and she had to turn to look at him. For the first time, standing a step above him, she felt they were equally matched, but the soft glint in his eyes nonetheless made her uneasy. 'I've often wondered how it was accomplished. Were they walking along, like this, and did she turn to face him, like you've done, and did his arm steal around her waist, like this . . .'

Dawn stepped backwards, almost tripped on the upward step, and regained her footing by flinging her hand out against the wall. She was annoyed to see laughter dancing in his eyes, but the seductive arm dropped to his side. 'You haven't a mind for scientific exploration, Miss Morrison? How disappointing! I was hoping you would help me solve the puzzle.'

She said haughtily, 'As far as I can see there's no puzzle at all. Obviously, your ancestors were either midgets or acrobats. It's far too cramped in here for two grown people to even conduct a pleasant conversation, much less ...' She broke off, and blushed, grateful that the dimness hid her colour.

He took the two steps in one so that he was standing beside her, very close, once again overpowering her with his size. She felt the warm brush of his breath across her cheek, his hand light upon her arm, and, worst of all, the ever-so-slight pressure of his chest against her breasts, titillating, embarrassing, and, in these cramped quarters, completely impossible to avoid. 'Ah,' he said softly, 'but you're forgetting my family's reputation as lovers. Passion requires very little room.'

'I, on the other hand,' she managed, turning quickly to resume her ascent, 'require a great deal of room, and this place is beginning to get a little claustrophobic.'

She heard his soft laughter follow her and once again her cheeks burned, but he said nothing further until they emerged through a doorway on to a light, airy hall. It was parquet-floored, panelled in natural pine, and lit with two oversized casement windows at either end. 'These are the modern apartments,' he said, and Dawn was amazed at the abrupt alteration in his tone. Once again he was at a distance, formal, and faintly contemptuous. 'The guest rooms. There are twelve altogether, and at a charge of fifty American dollars a night we should turn quite a hefty little profit, wouldn't you say?'

She was uncertain how to respond to this new mood, but did venture, 'It's very nice.'

'You think it will appeal to the rich American tourist, then? Of course we realise that when travelling abroad they do expect to experience some inconveniences—it wouldn't be Europe if they didn't!—so we've installed only three bathrooms on this floor.' He tipped his head towards her mockingly, his eyes bitter. 'But perhaps that's going a bit overboard? Would one have been sufficient?'

Dawn went cold under his sudden and totally undeserved hostility, and she replied, 'I'm sure I'm no expert on conducting a business such as this. I'm here merely to photograph and report what I see.'

'Then you may report,' he said with sudden harsh ferocity, 'that Byron Boyd has no desire to see a bunch of damn fools tramping over his property and lolling about his house in their Bermuda shorts and Polaroid cameras, so if they come they'd better be blasted sure to stay out of my way!'

She stared at him, aghast. 'If you'll forgive me for saying so, that's hardly the attitude to persuade the public to pay your outrageous fees and put Falkone's Acres at the head of their "must see" list on their next trip to Scotland! One doesn't go to all the trouble and expense of planning a vacation such as this merely to be insulted, any more than I would think you would go to all the expense of opening your house to the public simply for the sheer delight of ordering them from your doorstep.'

For a moment he glared at her with all the violence he might have liked to display to those crass and arrogant tourists he held in such contempt. He said curtly, 'No, I will not forgive you for saying so. And the word is "home", Miss Morrison. Not "house".' Then, with a lift of those powerful shoulders, the angry mood vanished as quickly as it had come. 'What the hell! It's done, now, and there's nothing but to make the best of it. Obviously, I should have left the role of tour guide to my sister.'

Dawn could not help murmuring in agreement, 'Obviously,' as she followed him down the hall, which bore a striking resemblance to the interior of any better-class American hotel. There were candle sconces on the wall, quality reproductions in strategic locations, gold brocade curtains at the windows. There was even, she noticed, a modern lift at one end. She must mark that down, it was something her readers would want to know, but she was having difficulty keeping her mind entirely on the article for pondering the puzzle of Byron Boyd. He had apparently gone to a great deal of trouble to make the place comfortable and appealing to the tourist, but went out of his way to let her know the extent of his distaste for the entire project. Each moment he was becoming more of an enigma, and each moment her desire was heightening to know more about him.

'These are all guest rooms along here,' he said, and opened the door to one. 'They're basically the same. Feel free to photograph any you like.'

She glanced inside at a large, tastefully decorated room, done in green and white wallpaper, dominated by a huge four-poster bed in the centre and a fireplace on the opposite wall. 'Do they all have fireplaces?' she asked, taking out her notebook.

'It stays a little chilly here all year round. Best way to cut the heating costs.' He opened another door. 'Bath.' She had a glimpse of blue tiles and modern facilities before he closed the door again.

She enquired, 'Where does the family sleep?' and

the sudden twinkle in his eyes made her want to
bite her tongue.

'Ah,' he murmured, 'a very astute question, and
one I'm most happy to answer.' He led the way
around a corner and through a small, tan door, up
another narrow flight of stairs, much shorter than
the last, and through another door.

Dawn protested, 'I didn't mean you should go
to the trouble of taking me there.'

He replied, 'No trouble at all. You see,' he
glanced over his shoulder with a slight, provocative
smile, 'fate has happily arranged it that your
bedchamber should be directly across the hall
from mine.'

Swallowing her discomfiture, she followed him
down a windowless stone corridor dimly lit with
electric lamps in amber sconces. Though the faint
lingering odour of paint and cleaning fluid
suggested this part of the house had also recently
been renovated, it was obviously much older, and
a more authentic sample of castle life. The floors
were stone, the portraits on these walls original
and faded with age, and the tapestries, one
particularly enormous one of the Lord's Supper,
she imagined were priceless. Byron paused with
one more reversion into his tour-master's tone to
explain, following the direction of her gaze, 'That
one dates back to the fourteenth century, done by
the mistress of the castle while her husband was
away at wars. It was a common occupation back
then, when the men were often away ten and
twenty years at a time, for the women to fill the
hours creating works of art. It was an altarcloth,
rescued from the chapel when the old place finally
tumbled down in the eighteenth century. It's a
little the worse for wear, I'm afraid.'

Dawn gazed at it admiringly, but dared not touch. She had been warned to ask permission before snapping any antiquities, as some proprietors were very peculiar about the damage flashbulbs could do to ancient artefacts. As she was on the verge of doing so, Byron moved away from her and swung open the large wooden door to another room.

She almost made the mistake of following him, thinking she was being escorted to her own room. But on the threshold she paused as he stepped inside. It was very obviously a man's room, filled with dark wood and the scent of sandalwood and a spicy cologne—the same scent, she noticed immediately, that he now wore. It was enormous, a king's chamber, one area arranged with comfortable couches and chairs, book stands and a writing desk, another filled with a huge, curtained pedestal bed, a black oak wardrobe, dressing-table and bureau. It made her uncomfortable, being in a man's bedroom, because to her the bedroom epitomised what was most private and individual about a person, and perhaps the feeling was intensified by the way he stood there, smiling in that faintly challenging way, his hand extended to invite her in. She refused to move.

He said, 'I assure you, I won't bite ... not at this stage of our relationship, anyway.' Dawn stiffened, and the reaction seemed to delight him. 'Come in, we'll have a pot of tea sent up and really get to know each other, shall we?'

She said, coldly but politely, 'Thank you, I would prefer to be shown to my own room now, please.'

His expression changed subtly, although whether it reflected amusement or annoyance she could not be certain. 'Strange,' he murmured. 'I was so certain it was *my* room you wanted to see.' He moved towards her and she stepped quickly out of his way, bristling at his deliberate misinterpretation of her motives. But he did not touch her. 'At any rate,' he tossed lightly over his shoulder as he moved across the hall to another door, 'now you know where it is, should you ever need to find it again.'

She replied, clasping her hands tightly together to control her tone, 'I doubt very much that such an occasion will ever come up.'

She reached the door just as she thought he would open it; he did not, but turned to lean over her with one arm propped on the frame, his eyes glinting softly. 'Ah, but my dear Miss Morrison, you are premature in your judgment of the future. All things are possible in Scotland, the land of romance and adventure.'

Deliberately, she reached beneath his arm and opened the door. She was glad that he spared her the awkwardness of ducking beneath him to enter the room by moving easily aside to allow her to pass. 'I hope you'll be comfortable here,' he said. 'These are prestige quarters—for very important guests. But for you,' again a challenging glance, 'only the best. You're commissioned to write a glowing description of our promise as a tourist trap and we must of course do everything within our power to make that task easier for you.'

'I'm assigned,' she corrected, walking away from him, 'to give an unbiased report on what I see here, and no inducement of yours will make me do otherwise.' But so far she had seen nothing to indicate that report would be anything other than favourable, and this room was no exception.

It was a semi-circular room, the walls were covered in a gold-flocked paper with matching brocade curtains and a carpet of a similar hue underfoot. The cherrywood furniture was elegant and gleamed softly in the light of one lamp and a low-burning fire. She stepped up to the window embrasure and looked out on a portion of the lake and a splendid, beautifully sculpted garden of clipped hedges and neat, colourful beds. She turned. 'Is this a tower room?'

'The entire floor is a tower,' he explained. 'This is only part. My room and yours, you see, were at one time joined into a single, massive chamber. Alas for its present-day occupants, they are now separated by a corridor and doors with locks.'

She almost smiled. Really, he was offensive and crude, but there was something rather charming in the offhanded way he made those unexpected passes—almost as though he were laughing at himself while baiting her.

'Of course you will see the rest of the castle,' he continued in the most casual tone. 'Feel free to explore at your leisure.' He passed by her on his way to the door, a peculiar half-smile on his lips. 'Of course,' he added politely, 'for a very special guest, I imagine I could arrange a private tour. By candlelight, of course. Ghost-ridden chambers and legend-filled halls should never be viewed by anything other than candlelight.'

She protested quickly, 'I wouldn't dream of imposing——'

He lifted a finger in light warning. 'It's a promise. And the Boyd clan is renowned for keeping its promises.'

The door closed behind him and Dawn was left in the elegant gold room, half of her hoping that

was one promise he would forget, half of her
hoping he would not. And she justified both of
them by telling herself it was only in the interest of
the article that she should care at all.

Deliberately, she began unpacking, moving back
and forth across the padded carpet from suitcase
to drawers to armoir, busily making plans for the
rest of the day. She could manage the self-assured
Mr Boyd, if need be, and despite his protestations
to the contrary, he must be as eager to have the
article in print as she was, or else she would never
have been invited. That guaranteed a certain
amount of co-operation on his part, and as long as
she maintained a clearly businesslike tone to their
dealings there was no reason to believe he would
not do the same. She would begin, she decided, by
taking afternoon shots of the castle façade, when
the light would lend a particularly romantic aura
to the whole, and intersperse some views of the
lake and the colourful garden.

But when Maggie brought up what the English
call 'high tea'—a substantial luncheon of cold
sliced turkey and watercress sandwiches accom-
panied by the ever-present pot of steaming black
tea—she began to yawn, and even Maggie noticed
she was succumbing to the unaccustomed effects
of jet lag. She kindly suggested that she lie down
for a while before dinner, and when she was gone
Dawn stretched out on the cushiony softness of
the white satin coverlet, telling herself it was only
for a few minutes, and fell immediately into a deep
and dreamless sleep.

She started when the maid tapped lightly on the
door, announcing dinner in half an hour, and sat
up on the bed, disorientated for a moment and
looking in some confusion about her. Darkness

had come through the drawn-back curtains, the
fire had burned down, but the lamp still glowed
warmly. A glance at her watch told her it was
seven-thirty. She got up quickly and began to strip
off her rumpled travelling suit.

She stood before the wardrobe in her under-
things, looking with some criticism at the selection
of clothes she had brought with her—sensible
suits, plain shirtwaisters and skirts, a few
singularly unattractive dresses. For the first time
she wished she had brought something a little
more festive—the sheer white blouse with its
Victorian collar and cascades of lace, the yellow
voile with the plunging neckline and billowing
skirt, the clinging aqua knit . . . all of which she
had bought on impulse and hardly ever wore.

With a sigh she finally selected a white wool,
plain and simple except for the delicately scooped
neckline and full, puffed sleeves. It was a light
fabric, pleated at the bodice to flow about her
figure sensuously as she moved, and reserved
strictly for social occasions. She did not know why
she should regard her first dinner across the table
from the subject of her research as a social
occasion.

She spent little time on make-up—with the
pressures of her career she had soon learned she
simply did not have it to spare—but applied a
touch of blusher to her cheeks, a crease of shadow
to deepen her naturally large eyes, a pale shade of
lip-gloss. Then she sat before the dressing table
and unbound her hair, brushing it forward over
her shoulder, and for the briefest moment had the
wild notion to wear it loose tonight.

Sternly, she reprimanded herself, and wound it
into a tight knot at the nape of her neck. She

would never make a professional woman if she allowed herself to be transported into whims of romance by every new place she visited!

In completion of her toilette she fastened a thin gold chain about her neck and stepped out into the corridor, for a moment facing confusion about which way to turn. Fortunately, she was spared that decision by the emergence at that same moment of Byron from his room across the way, and he only stood there, looking at her, until she felt a tingle of embarrassment add to the artificial blush on her cheeks.

He examined her with the experienced eye of a connoisseur of women, and she found herself wishing she had chosen instead the plain navy knit with its straight lines and high collar. When, as he closed his door, the slight draught it created moved the fabric gently against her body, outlining each detail from the soft swelling of breasts to flat abdomen to slender thighs, she thought his eyes missed nothing. And the appreciative light there confirmed her suspicions as he moved towards her and said softly. 'The transformation is an improvement.'

She replied, 'Thank you very much, I'm sure, but I wasn't seeking your approval.'

'Oh, yes, you were. Every woman dresses for the approval of a man. It's the natural order of things.'

The fact that, on this occasion, she harboured a vague and annoying suspicion that he was right only added to her indignation and she jerked angrily away from his protective hand on her elbow. 'Can't you come near a person without touching?' she demanded.

'It's a weakness of mine,' he admitted, calmly

replacing his hand with a more dominant grip, 'which strangely only manifests itself in the presence of women.'

Dawn glanced at him, and wondered if the philosophy of a woman's dressing habits could be applied to men as well, for the transformation in him, too, had been an improvement. He wore a dark grey suit that set off his powerful shoulders and slim waist to such perfection there was no doubt it was tailored specifically to fit his form; the silk tie he wore was a becoming shade of light blue ornamented with a modest, though lustrous, pearl stick pin. The handkerchief in his pocket matched the tie, and his shirt was of such a pale blue as to be almost white, like a spring sky overcast with translucent clouds. His dark hair was thick and glossy and framed a face which, she was surprised to notice, could be almost handsome in its austerity.

They took the lift down, and its silent motion and padded interior made their confinement seem almost too close. The little room was filled with the faint, aromatic scent of Byron's cologne which she found both alluring and distinctively his own. Her entire range of vision was dominated by him, every sense touched by him, and she knew she would not have been so uncomfortable had he in any way been less essentially masculine. Unconsciously, she began to inch away, and he glanced at her in amusement. 'You *do* have claustrophobia, don't you? That must be very awkward for you in—er—' he lifted his brow suggestively, 'intimate social situations.'

Dawn lifted her chin and stared defiantly straight ahead, saying nothing until the lift bounced to a gentle stop. 'You'll have to get lost a few times before you begin to know your way around,' he said as they stepped out into the foyer. 'Of course, if you prefer to play it safe you can always take the lift.' He glanced at her. 'Do you like to play it safe, Miss Morrison?'

She replied, following him through the tiled corridor and into a warm, richly scarlet anteroom, 'Where business matters are concerned, yes.'

He paused and gestured her to precede him into the room. 'Are there ever any other matters in your life besides business, I wonder?' he drawled, and she did not reply, because Maggie was there before them and turned with a warm greeting.

'Oh, there you are. You made it with no trouble, I see. We just have time for a drink before dinner, so come, let's relax a minute. Did you have a nice rest?'

'Very nice, thank you,' Dawn replied as a cool glass of amber liquid was pressed into her hand, and she was unconsciously relieved for the presence of Maggie between herself and Byron. 'I'm only sorry that a whole afternoon has gone by, and there was so much I wanted to do.'

'There's plenty of time for that,' said Byron, filling his own glass, and turned to her with a salute. 'A toast. To the beginning of a profitable venture for all of us.'

Dawn smiled politely, but could not help wondering how he could change so drastically from one mood to the other, and whether or not his toast was meant facetiously.

'Why, Miss Morrison,' he commented in some surprise, 'You're not drinking. Don't you approve the toast?'

'I don't drink—much,' she answered, and searched for a table upon which to set her drink.

'How refreshing,' he murmured, observing her through narrowed eyes. 'And also a little insulting. You see, this family has been producing the best Scotch whisky in the Hebrides for over five generations, and war has been declared before on men who refused a drink in this house.'

Maggie declared, 'Oh Byron, really you're being rude.'

'Again,' he enquired lightly, 'or still?'

Maggie ingnored him, turning back to Dawn. 'What do you think of what you've seen so far? How do you think it will appeal to your readers?'

'It's marvellous,' Dawn replied enthusiastically, although she knew that, empirically, she had very little data upon which to base such an unqualified review. 'The guest rooms are very comfortable and tasteful, and the grounds are simply breathtaking. The castle—what I've seen of it so far—has such wonderful character, without the musty feeling one finds in so many old houses. I think your guests will be delighted with the accommodations and charmed by the atmosphere, and will gladly come again and again.'

'Perhaps we could ensure that,' suggested Byron, 'by staging a little entertainment here and there. Nothing elaborate, you understand, just a note of local colour. We could bring the natives in their plumes and feathers to do a dance every evening in the back garden. And, as a special bonus on Saturday night, how about a regiment in full Highland battle dress to stage a raid on the old place? Complete with bloody sabres and ear-splitting shrieks and maybe a maiden or two carried off for good measure. Your fat old widows would be quivering in their diamond-studded slippers and loving every minute of it.' Again the

sharp note of bitterness in his voice as he turned
abruptly to lift the glass to his lips, and Dawn
had restrained herself long enough.

'Do you have a prejudice against Americans in
general,' she demanded, 'or simply American
tourists? And is your bigotry limited to tourists, or
does it extend to include all mankind?'

At first he lookd startled, then his eyes
narrowed ominously as he scrutinised her. 'As a
matter of fact,' he said coolly, 'my "bigotry" as
you choose to call it, extends only to that group of
impertinent, money-grubbing rabble who force
themselves into my home and invade my privacy.'

Which included her, she realised with a start.
She belonged to the lowest class of money-
grubbing tourist in his mind, for not only was she
invading his domain and taking advantage of his
hospitality, but she was encouraging others to do
the same—and for the indisputably banal purpose
of selling more magazines. That explained if
nothing else did, his domineering, mocking, faintly
contemptuous attitude towards her, and she
thought that was blatantly unfair.

Maggie said somewhat uncomfortably, 'As
you've probably guessed, it wasn't Byron's idea to
open the house. I just thought it would be such a
good idea—there's so much of the charm of the
islands no one ever knows about—and I *do* think
it will bring in a nice income . . . '

'Stars above!' he exclaimed in exasperation.
'As though it was necessary! What you'll make
here in a year won't even pay the export taxes
on my whisky for a single month. Money is no
excuse.'

'I can understand how you feel,' ventured
Dawn.

He turned on her. 'You can't possibly understand how I feel! This fortress has stood inviolate
against outsiders for over five centuries—I can see
no reason to surrender now in the name of
progress. We islanders are an exclusive people,' he
explained, somewhat more patiently. 'We hold our
privacy very highly. The entire concept of bringing
boatloads of tourists in to swarm all over the
island violates a sacred heritage of our people—
and we're very proud of our heritage.'

Dawn continued, firmly, 'I understand how you
feel. But don't you think you're being a little
selfish?'

'If I am,' he replied, 'it's my right.'

She tried a different tactic. 'The people who
come here,' she said, 'will come in search of
a different way of life. A small, untouched part
of the world that can have for them, for a time,
a very special meaning. There are so few places
like that left on this planet. I don't think anyone has the right to keep one entirely to himself.'

For a moment she almost thought her argument
touched a valid note with him, but then he said,
'And your solution to that is to bring in more and
more people to desecrate what little there is left
that's untouched by the outside world?'

She shook her head. 'Why must you persist
upon assuming they'll desecrate anything? They
don't want to destroy your way of life—only share
in it for a moment! This castle—so rich in Scottish
history—things the textbooks don't record. The
beautiful works of art locked up here—never to be
seen by anyone but yourself. How could you—
why could you *want* to—keep all this away from
the rest of the world?'

From far away she heard a telephone ring down the hall. Discreetly, Maggie, slipped out to answer it.

Byron looked at her for a time, and gradually she noticed his features soften, perhaps a faint hint of a smile in his eyes. 'You've been here for such a short time—you've seen so little of the castle or the island, but you speak as though you know it, You make a very persuasive devil's advocate, Miss Morrison, and I almost think you could make me change my mind. But then,' he added, his eyes softly raking her from bosom to calf, 'given half a chance I imagine you could change any man's mind about almost anything. That's your advantage in being born a female, and such a delightfully constructed one at that.'

Dawn almost stamped her foot in impatience. 'It doesn't require a feminine body,' she told him, 'to see the logic in what I'm saying. But perhaps it does require a male mind to *refuse* to see it and hide behind flimsy evasions and irrelevant and ineffective flattery.'

Immediately she could have bitten her tongue, watching as the echoes of her words died away and his eyes darkened and grew remote. The air between them was static as he cautioned , 'Careful, Miss Morrison. Your chauvinism is showing!'

The electric moment was broken by the re-entrance of Maggie, and Dawn turned abruptly away from her, her cheeks flaming, once again cursing herself for that uncontrollable temper which would one day cost her a job. She only hoped, with sudden desperation, that it would not be this one.

'It's for you, Byron,' Maggie said quietly. 'Thomas.'

A pause, then he said curtly, 'Doesn't he know it's the dinner hour?'

'He said it was important.'

He set his glass down on the table and stalked towards the door. There he turned back, however, and said smoothly, 'I'm so sorry you find my flattery ineffective, Miss Morrison, I shall try to do better in the future.'

'Business, you know,' explained Maggie when he was gone. 'Thomas Mann is Byron's partner in the distillery.'

Dawn smiled in what she hoped was an understanding manner, and appreciated the chance to let her cheeks cool. Although the telephone was some distance away from the room in which they were seated, it was impossible to ignore the sound of Byron's voice, growing louder and more heated as the minutes ticked on. The two women could only look at one another uncomfortably, trying to smile, though rather weakly, trying to pretend nothing was amiss.

In a matter of moments Byron reappeared at the door, his trench coat flung over his arm, his dark face suffused with a choleric tint. 'Don't count on me for dinner,' he said curtly. 'I don't know how late I'll be.' And, after a few striding footsteps, they heard the front door slam.

Maggie glanced at her apologetically, and Dawn was aware of a vast disappointment that he was gone. Mostly she was thinking, angry and impatient with both herself and the circumstances, 'What rotten timing! Just when we were beginning to communicate!'

CHAPTER THREE

WHEN Maggie only stood there, looking after him, moment after anxious moment, Dawn felt it was important to say something. She ventured, 'I do hope it's nothing serious.'

Maggie sighed, and dragged her eyes away from the empty doorway to focus on Dawn. She said, 'I suppose you're entitled to some explanation.' For a moment she looked as though debating what to tell her, and when, and if at all. Then, with an abrupt resumption of her brisk efficiency, she decided, 'What matter, you'll hear the gossip sooner or later. Come along then, let's go in to dinner, and I'll see what I can do to excuse my brother's abominable behaviour.'

As they walked through two, or perhaps three, stone corridors, Dawn anxiously divided her attention on trying to make note of her surroundings so that she might find her way back again, and listening to what Maggie was saying. Soon she lost interest altogether in the making of a mental map for total absorption in the subject of her discourse.

'I know it's no excuse,' Maggie was saying, 'but Byron has problems right now—business and personal. He's not usually quite so ill-mannered, or short-spoken, with strangers ... although he can be when the mood strikes him or he takes one of his inexplicable dislikes ...!' She glanced at her anxiously and added quickly, 'Which is not the case with you, I assure you, if only you'll allow me to explain ...'

Dawn shook her head sadly and tried to smile through a dry spot in her throat. 'But I'm very much afraid it is, Maggie. I think I represent to your brother all that he most dislikes—the threat to his "fortress", as he likes to call it, and he retaliates to me exactly the way he would like to do to a busload of tourists ... Don't worry,' she assured her, 'it won't influence my piece at all.' She smiled a little. 'There's no room in my outline for a personal opinion of the proprietor of the establishment!'

Maggie shook her head. 'It's true, you know, that Byron was against this entire idea from the beginning, but he was very tolerant with me, and I thought, until recently, he might even eventually adjust ... But that's not really the problem, you see ...'

By this time they had entered a moss green dining room, very cosy and not overly large, and she interrupted herself to explain, 'This's not, of course, where we will seat our guests. This is the family dining area, the Great Hall has a banquet table and a seating capacity of fifty, and I had intended a true medieval flavour with the evening meal, with torches on the wall and perhaps period costumes ...' She gestured her to be seated and Dawn slipped into a carved oak chair with green velvet padding while Maggie murmured something to the maid and the place setting at the head of the table was removed.

Tactfully, Maggie did not continue the conversation until the soup was brought, a rich, flavourful broth, laced, Dawn noticed in some surprise, with what appeared to be whisky. It was surprisingly very good. 'You see,' Maggie resumed somewhat reluctantly as the maid withdrew and the heavy oak doors were pulled discreetly closed behind her, 'there's a problem with the distillery ... Thomas Mann is Byron's partner. He was in partnership with our father before Byron inherited, so you see it's a long-standing—and very profitable—arrangement. But ...' She dropped her eyes briefly. 'Thomas has a daughter, Hilary. She and Byron were engaged to be married, but only last week she broke it off.'

The candelabra in the centre of the table seemed to gleam less brightly, the dark panelling around the room seemed to harbour more shadows, the heavy moss velvet curtains seemed less elegant than funereal. Dawn was not certain she wanted to hear more. After all, it was none of her concern. Her limits were to architecture, accommodation, meals and entertainment. The personality and personal problems of her host had nothing to do with her assignment. Yet she took another sip of her soup and did nothing to discourage Maggie from continuing.

'Above all,' said Maggie, fastening her intensely with her eyes, 'Byron values loyalty. He's very strict about that in his dealings with others and there can be no compromises. It's—rather of a family trait, you see. What Hilary did was unforgivable.' A man who had succeeded to his heritage through five centuries of fiercely loyal and domineering rulers of the island would have those characteristics, thought Dawn. Unbreakable pride, and unswerving distaste for anyone who dealt with him less than honestly. It was understandable.

Maggie kept her eyes on her soup, dipping the spoon in and out and letting the liquid slide back into the bowl without ever lifting it above the rim. 'Perhaps you can understand if his attitude with all women is a little hostile now—even with me! He was deeply hurt.'

Dawn said, 'Certainly I understand, and as I told you before, none of this will influence me in the least.'

Maggie sighed. 'It's likely to go on for some time. You see, Byron has some foolish notion in his head about severing all dealings with the Manns. . . .'

'But he surely can't let his personal life influence business decisions!' Dawn cried, and reminded herself a moment too late that it was none of her business.

Maggie tilted her head slightly, as though half in agreement. 'But you see, Hilary will eventually inherit everything that's her father's—including his interest in the distillery. Even now, she holds an executive position with enormous decision-making powers. Byron simply refuses to deal with her; he doesn't trust her.'

Part of Dawn understood his position, another part insisted that a woman should not be judged in the business world according to the way she managed her personal life. The other part told her sternly, once again, that it was none of her concern.

'Until now, Byron has refused to deal with either of them except through his lawyers. He wouldn't even go to Thomas's house for fear of running into Hilary in some situation where he couldn't close his office door on her or crowd her out with other people. But now . . .' she looked slightly encouraged, 'perhaps his going over there tonight means he's softening a little, and is ready to start acting civilised again.'

Remembering the look on Byron's face as he had left, Dawn did not think a desire for civilised behaviour was one of his driving motives, but Maggie obviously knew him better than she did. Perhaps the colour in his face and the tension in his carriage had not been anger at all, but passion. And perhaps his leaving his dinner guest—if Dawn could properly refer to herself as that—and rushing to the side of his former fiancée meant their little quarrel would be patched up, and everyone would live happily ever after.

It really did not concern her.

With the next course, flaked baked trout which Maggie told her had been caught only that morning in a nearby stream, they moved on to lighter subjects, and Dawn recalled little that was said. Perhaps they discussed a little of Maggie's plans concerning the itinerary and projected summer opening, but it was desultory table conversation, nothing Dawn could not get down in her notebook in detail later on. She found herself keeping an eye on the polished grandfather clock in the corner, and as the hour passed and they rose from the table, she thought the reunion must be going very well. After all, Byron had said he did not know how late he would be. Perhaps he would not be back at all tonight.

And it was not as though she would really notice whether he was or not. What business she had with him—finding a guide to show her about the island, requesting permission to photograph some of his works of art—could very easily wait until morning.

Maggie took her through the downstairs rooms, switching on lights as they went—library, sitting rooms, a large, efficient office which once again smelled hauntingly of Byron's cologne, passage-ways and staircases winding up and down, and it was all a maze to Dawn. 'You need to get a map for your guests!' she laughed.

Maggie smiled. 'They're being printed now.' Then, 'Of course you realise this floor is an extension of the family living quarters. The upper floor will belong to the guests, with its Great Hall for dining and lounging, their own rooms just around the corner, and the exhibitions right above.'

'The architecture,' mused Dawn, as they made their way back towards the foyer, 'is strange. It's not at all like I expected to find in a castle. It all seems so—well planned, and convenient.'

Maggie laughed. 'I'm glad you think so, because that impression is achieved as the result of five generations of enterprising Boyds, too stubborn to leave their ancestral home, too fond of luxury to put up with the inconveniences of castle life. Of course you realise what we're standing in now is no older than three centuries, and when it was rebuilt I believe there was a French bride who brought many progressive ideas on architecture to the island from her homeland.'

'What parts remain of the original structure?'

'The dungeons, of course, although no one ever goes down there. The two towers on the front— they're going to be open for exhibition. You can see there the marks made by cannonballs on the stone, the powder burns, the little slits in the walls through which the archers used to fire, and the spiral stairways which made it almost impossible for an enemy to wage an offensive attack, and very easy for the lord of the castle to defend. In one of these is the scarred railing Byron told you about.'

'Naturally, I'll want to photograph that.' As they reached the elevator Dawn reached out lightly to graze a cold stone wall. 'How long has the castle been here?' she asked again.

'Five centuries,' replied Maggie proudly.

The girl shook her head in amazement. To Dawn, who had not lived in any one place for more than a year at a time since her parents' divorce when she was in high school, such permanence and stability was a matter of the sheerest wonder.

At ten o'clock Maggie walked her back to her room and they said goodnight. She felt she should be tired, so she dressed for bed, and even went so far as to turn back the puffy satin coverlet before she realised the extensive nap she had taken that afternoon had completely eliminated any possibility of sleep in the immediate future.

Though conservative in her daytime wear, Dawn was extravagant with nightclothes. Tonight, despite the chilly spring evening, she wore a sheer white nylon peignoir printed all over with tiny blue flowers. The inner garment was sleeveless and cut low across the bosom, fastened from bodice to waist with only three small blue ribbons, which left a great amount of bare flesh exposed. The outer garment, which she slipped on now as she padded across the carpeted room to the window seat, though it had full, long sleeves and a cascade of lace around the shoulders, fastened with only one ribbon at the top and could in no way be considered modest.

She took up the brush and began to stroke her hair into long cords as she sat in the window seat and gazed out across the still and silent garden. The moon was so bright it was almost like day, brushed with the special softness only a full moon can bring. Every detail of the garden was clear, the colours, the glowing stones of the path, even the reflection of the still castle rippling in the lake. And that gave her a sudden idea.

Night shots were especially effective, and if she could capture this setting in this once-in-a-lifetime manifestation of moonlight, the accomplishment would not only impress her editor beyond measure but possibly even merit submission to higher authorities—perhaps to be considered for one of the coveted photographers' awards. It was too good an opportunity to miss.

Because timing was very important where natural lighting was concerned, and because she did not think anyone would be about at this hour, it did not occur to her to stop and dress, or even throw a light coat over her shoulders. She merely plunged her bare feet into satin slippers, swept up her equipment, and stole out into the hall towards the lift.

The lift deposited her right where she wanted to be—in the front foyer, and she rememberd Byron's jeering words, 'Do you like to play it safe, Miss Morrison?' As she made her way through the dimly lit foyer and pulled open the front door she told herself sternly that in the dead of night in an unfamiliar environment the only sensible thing to do was to play it safe. It did not occur to her that she was at that moment doing exactly the opposite.

First, she found the path which led around the side of the house to the garden, stumbling a little, scuffing her slippers and her exposed toes on the stones. Strange, it had seemed much brighter from her window. She supposed the oaks cut out a great deal of the light as it made its way towards the ground, giving the illusion of brilliance from a height, when in fact it was dark and shadowy on the ground.

As she came into the high hedges of the garden she was acutely disappointed. From the ground angle, there was none of that lustrous brilliance bathing the garden which she had remarked from her window. The hedges were at least six feet tall, overshadowing the beds, even dulling the curving stone walkways. Only the little fountain in the centre still sparkled whiteness, and it was a very ordinary fountain. Dawn placed her camera bag on a low stone bench and then sat down beside it, looking about her discontentedly.

The night was still and peaceful, beautiful despite its lack of photogenic capability, and she would have liked to have sat there a while longer. But it was chilly, a slight breeze blew across the lake and caused her to shiver; she was suddenly aware that the stone bench was very cold against her scantily-protected thighs.

She started to rise, but then stopped in mid-motion at the sound of voices and motion— unaccountably very close, and getting closer, having apparently materialised out of nowhere.

'It was very foolish of you, Hilary, to have followed me here.' It was Byron's voice, clipped, authoritative; he was obviously keeping his temper under control with great difficulty. 'I thought I made it quite clear this evening that we have nothing to discuss.'

Wildly, Dawn looked about her. Her position was well shielded by the hedges, but it offered the disadvantage of limiting her range of vision as well, so that the couple might stumble upon her at any moment without warning, and there was no place to hide. How had they got here so quickly?

Where *had* they come from? Then she remembered viewing from one of the upstairs windows a small building which might have been a garage, towards the back, and naturally Byron would take the short cut through the garden to reach the nearest entrance. The bulk of the castle itself would have hidden the sounds from her until they were almost upon her. She shrank down and tried to make herself invisible. Of all the unimagined horrors, to be discovered by the two of them, sitting here in her nightgown—eavesdropping!

'And I thought *I* made it quite clear that I wouldn't let you out of my sight tonight until we got this thing straightened out!' A woman's voice now, perhaps not quite as angry, but every bit as determined. Her tone was well-bred and sophisticated, despite the rapid rush of words, faintly hinting of the refinement of an English finishing school. Dawn could almost form a mental picture of her, and then swiftly reprimanded herself for it. But she could not help listening.

'Since when,' he asked dryly, 'did you become a woman of your word?'

A pause, and then the low drawl, 'I think I just remembered what I dislike most about you, darling.'

'Good. Then perhaps you also remember why I find it necessary to sever all aspects of our relationship—permanently.'

'You're overbearing, domineering, selfish and completely impossible to love. But you're a damn good businessman and I can't stand by and watch you——'

'If it pains you so, I suggest you don't watch. Allow your father to sign over his interest to me and we can all wash our hands of one another for good.'

'You expect people to be wind-up toys!' Hilary cried. 'You're so used to being lord and master—so full of nonsensical tradition about being ruler of the island—you think you can control people's emotions. You tried to make me into something I wasn't, and when it didn't work you expected——'

'All I ever expected from you,' Byron returned coldly, 'was fidelity.'

'That,' she retaliated sharply, 'was too much. If you consider the circumstances . . .'

He laughed bitterly. 'Ah, yes, the circumstances. It's no use, Hilary. You can stand here and justify and rationalise and offer excuses until we're both old and grey and none of them will change what has happened. I only hope that poor old Marcus never realises what a bad bargain he's got, and that the next time you decide to go to bed with another man, you'll at least have the courtesy not to brag to your fiancé about it!'

There was the sharp report of flesh against flesh, cracking through the stillness like a shot. Dawn winced and jumped, and then, as the echoes died away, she could hear the sounds of breathing so close it seemed they were directly above her, on the other side of the hedge. He said in a low voice. 'I think that appropriately concludes a very inappropriate conversation. Goodnight, Hilary.'

In a moment there was the sound of light, rapid, retreating footsteps, and then silence. Dawn waited in frozen stillness, hardly daring to breathe, until she heard a second pair of footsteps on the path beside her, moving past her, abruptly disappearing as though Byron had stepped on to the grass as the shortest route to the house.

With a sigh of relief, she rose and moved out of her hiding place—directly into his path.

He towered over her, his eyes two dark, glittering slits, the moonlight just bright enough to show the dark splash of colour across one side of his face which her hand had left, the sound of his breathing, over-loud and a little uneven, reaching her easily across the distance of a few feet which separated them. At some point during the evening he had removed his tie and unbuttoned his collar, and she could see the little beads of perspiration gleaming on the tuft of dark hair at his throat; every muscle in his body seemed to be coiled with tension, ready to spring.

'So,' he said, very softly, 'the fairy-spy is at it again.'

She tried not to shrink back, and defended hotly, 'If you would only let me explain . . . I came down here to take some pictures, and by the time I heard your voices you were on me . . . I couldn't very well step out from the hedges without it looking as though—as though——'

'As though you were spying,' he supplied with deceptive mildness. 'Which is, of course, exactly what you were doing.'

'I was not! I thought the garden was empty! I came to take pictures——'

He looked around him, hands outspread. 'Without a camera?'

Triumphantly, she marched back to the bench and produced the evidence.

Still, only a light, knowing smile altered his features as he moved around her to lounge casually on the bench. 'Well, in lieu of photographs, did you learn anything interesting?'

'I told you——'

Byron waved a hand negligently. 'Never mind what you told me. The point is . . .' His voice dropped in tone, the glow in his eyes was as gentle as the moonlight as they swept over her. 'Here we are alone in a moonlit garden, and you've so very thoughtfully dressed the part ... And I have decided to forgive your eavesdropping and your impertinence. It's a night for romance, Dawn.'

She was suddenly acutely aware of the night breeze billowing the filmy nightgown around her, and the way his bright eyes did not miss a detail. Every sense was alerted for what might happen next while every instinct warned her not to stay to find out. She said stiffly, 'I'm going inside.'

She turned to go and was stopped by his hand, lightly capturing one long strand of her silvery hair. 'Your hair,' he said softly, 'is magnificent.' She turned, and was surprised to see that the light in his eyes had deepened to something almost like amazement as he examined the strand of hair in the moonlight, his fingers turning and separating it, opening it to his delicate, almost worshipful scrutiny. His voice was low and husky, as though he spoke secret thoughts out loud, and this time there could be no doubt about the sincerity of his compliment. 'One of nature's wonders. Like wheat and flax growing together in the sun, blended by the wind ... You should always wear it that way.'

Dawn smiled uncertainly, and then his other hand came forward, threading through her hair at the temples, lifting it and watching it fall like a fluttering veil over her shoulders. His eyes were so dark, so mesmerising with that strange, intent light in their depths, that Dawn hardly felt the pressure that tilted her head back even as it drew her face closer to his. Only the sudden wild beating of her heart told her what was happening as he bent his head and she felt once again the touch of his lips upon hers.

As before, his kiss began with a promise, a delicate foretelling of pleasures to come. And it was that promise that captured Dawn, exposing her hidden vulnerabilities and brushing across the chords of passion with deceptive gentleness, lulling her into the security that the danger could be controlled, telling her the pleasure was worth the risk. But this time the kiss deepened with swift intent before she knew what was happening, before she had a chance to guard her emotions or her instincts against the unexpected response Byron was evoking. His arms closed around her with crushing strength, gathering her soft form into his hard one, his lips parted hers in deepening exploration and she melted against him, helpless to stop him or to resist, helpless to do anything but let the flare of electrified senses rule her head.

'Dawn,' he murmured against her mouth. 'Sweet Dawn ... fairy angel ...' Strong broad hands explored the length of her back, sweeping beneath her hair and threading through it, cupping and gathering and letting it fall again, while his lips dropped light electric kisses over her face and her neck. His breath seared her everywhere it touched, starting little flames that shivered throughout her until her own breathing was sporadic and the pounding of her heart shook her entire body. His hand drifted downwards to explore the curve of her waist through material so thin it might as well have been non-existent, then moved upwards again, ever upwards, until she felt the pressure of his palm cupping her breast.

She did not understand the wild and mind-stripping response that exploded within her, the tight yearning that built and weakened her, numbing her to everything except the aching need to draw him closer. She seemed to stop breathing altogether and she could no longer feel the painful beating of her heart. She could feel nothing but the presence of Byron, his hands upon her, and the need for him . . .

He whispered huskily, 'Dawn, love . . . Let's go inside—together.'

And then she remembered. Reason returned in a sudden cold sweep as she remembered angry voices, the fury in his eyes and the tension in his muscles when he discovered her. Hilary. He had come from Hilary to her. He was using her, as a release for built-up anger or as a balm to his ego after a fight with his fiancée . . . He had manipulated her with his expert sensuality and made her forget the promise she had made to herself, made her forget her purpose and her position here . . . He was using her for his own needs and had no thought of her own.

She pushed him away with all the force in her rubbery muscles. 'No!' It was meant to sound angry and determined, it came out as something hardly above a weak whisper. She turned away quickly and crossed her arms against the sudden chilling absence of him. She was shaking, but she determined not to let him see. She lifted her small chin defiantly and stared out over the lake which suddenly seemed cold and uninviting, like a sheet of dark glass. The air was chill, and his lingering warmth clung to her like a ghost, only making her shiver more.

She felt him, tense and silent, beside her. If he even breathed she could not hear it over her desperate struggle to regulate her own breathing and to subdue the thundering of her heart. The moments stretched out endlessly, and he did not move. She wanted to scream at him to leave her alone, but she knew she did not have the strength in her legs to get up and walk away from him.

More time passed, and Byron simply sat there, saying nothing, not moving. She could feel his anger as though it were a physical thing, quiet and low and eminently dangerous. At last she could stand it no longer. She made herself stand. She turned to go.

His voice was unexpectedly quiet behind her. 'How old are you, Dawn?'

She responded automatically, turning in some surprise, 'Twenty-five.' The steadiness of her voice amazed her. She was still shaking inside.

He rose, but made no move to approach her. His face was shadowed and his voice unreadable. 'I'm thirty-four, and I ask you to take the advice of someone older and wiser. Don't run around half-dressed in misty gardens looking to strike a romantic pose. These games men and women play—too often we find we no longer have control over how they will end.'

Dawn stood there a moment longer, speechless and uncertain. Then she caught up her skirts and went quickly back towards the castle. At that moment she did not know who she trusted less— Byron Boyd, or herself.

In the draughty foyer she stood for a moment, letting the stillness cool her cheeks and penetrate her tangled emotions. She did not know whether she should be insulted or angry, flattered or afraid. In fact, she did not know anything at all.

At last, hearing a far-away clock chime midnight, she turned towards the staircase she and Byron had used that afternoon. Something told her strongly it was too late for playing it safe tonight.

CHAPTER FOUR

MAGGIE had told her that breakfast was served buffet-style in the family dining room from seven until nine. She made only one wrong turn on her way down, but quickly discovered her mistake and retraced her steps by following the scents of methane chafing dishes and fresh coffee.

There was a young man there before her, blond, small of frame, and perhaps in his late twenties. He was serving himself from the sideboard of covered dishes, and when Dawn came in he looked up with a pleasant smile. 'Hello. You must be the young lady from the magazine.' He set aside his plate and extended his hand. 'I'm Vernon Marshall.'

She took his hand and returned his smile. 'Dawn Morrison.'

'Maggie has gone into town shopping, and she said I was to keep you company until Byron got back. The coffee is especially in your honour. Shall I pour you some?'

'Yes, please.' She accepted the cup and added, 'I imagine there's a great deal of traffic back and forth to Oban. Do you use the ferry, or a private boat?'

He laughed a little, shaking his head. 'Neither. The island is really quite self-sufficient. There's a very adequate little village of shops and businesses, and it's considered something of a slap in the face to the island's reputation for a native to go to the mainland for anything other than the sheerest necessary business.'

'I only arrived yesterday,' she explained. 'I know very little about the island.' She took her coffee cup and started for the table.

'What,' he protested, 'aren't you going to eat anything?'

'I'm not much for breakfast,' she admitted.

'Oh, but you'll be starving before midday if you don't. There's something about the air here that really works on a fellow's appetite. Come, there's bacon and kidneys and eggs—or chops if you prefer. No? Then you must at least try one of these honey-cakes. They're the main reason I came to the island four years ago and have had no desire to leave since.'

She let him place not one, but two, of the large, puffy, deliciously fragrant rolls on a plate for her, along with a generous scoop of creamy white butter. 'You're not a native, then?'

He shook his head, grinning, as he gestured her to preceed him to the table. 'Can't you tell? London. I worked for Byron's solicitors there until I heard he needed someone to manage his clerical affairs at the plant. Naturally, I jumped at the chance.'

Dawn sat down and bit into the soft golden crust of the roll and its exotic sweetness melted in her mouth. 'Umm,' she murmured, 'this is delicious!'

'Aren't they just? The recipe is an island secret. I told Byron if he manufactured those instead of whisky he would double his profits. He didn't think it was very funny.'

Dawn could imagine that. She had not discovered a sense of humour to be one of Byron's most striking attributes.

'This,' she told him beginning on the second

roll, 'will be a definite selling point to my readers. It's worth the fare just to taste one!'

He grinned in approval, as though she had just been accepted into some exclusive club. 'I expect this entire venture will be a big boost for business all over the island. I wouldn't be surprised if the gross income didn't double overnight—and I think sometimes that's the only reason Byron has gone along with the idea.'

Dawn was surprised. 'I don't understand what you mean.'

'Well, naturally, he feels responsible for the residents here. Everyone, in one way or another, owes their existence to Falkone's Distillery. When times are bad, he sees them through. When times are good, he shares the profits—rather like they did in the old days, when everyone on the island would take shelter behind the castle walls during an invasion.'

'I see,' she murmured, and sipped her coffee. Philanthropy was another attribute she would not have credited Byron with.

'I really think Falkone's Acres has a lot to offer as a holiday spot,' Vernon continued enthusiastically. 'Where else could you find so many different things in such a small area?' In a motion, he moved his chair closer to hers and began tracing an outline of the island on the tablecloth with his finger. She bent her head close to his to follow the pattern of a rough triangular crease in the linen. 'Of course, we're surrounded by a core of mountains, some of them climbable, and there are even a few brave enough to attempt some rough Nordic skiing in season. And at the base are those gorgeous lochs and streams practically crawling with fish. Here and there . . .' He made X's to the north and west. 'Are primeval forests which are a botanist's heaven, and of course, here, the castle with all its history and romance. And less than a mile away is the village, with a grocery and a chemist's and a cleaners—really all the conveniences of modern life. And it has a certain charm of its own, you know, with the cobbled streets and brightly painted shop fronts. There are definitely possibilities there for souvenir shops and maybe a guest house or two of its own.'

'I'll bet you have to fight Byron on that one,' she said, and he grinned.

'Tooth and nail,' he answered, and they laughed together softly as though over some shared secret.

'Well, I see the two of you are enjoying a nice cosy chat. Perhaps I shouldn't interrupt.'

Byron had entered the room, and his eyes passed from one to the other of them with a dark glance which made Dawn move away selfconsciously. He made her feel like a child caught with her hand in the cookie jar, and she resented it.

'Hello, Byron,' said Vernon cheerfully. 'I was just telling Dawn a little about the island.'

Byron went over to the sideboard and poured himself a cup of tea. 'Then perhaps you've found the perfect guide, Dawn,' he said, turning to view them over the rim of his cup. 'I'm sure touring the island must be high on your list of priorities ... especially if it's in the company of a knowledgeable and—amiable companion.'

He was dressed today in casual grey slacks and a cream shirt, cuffed up at the sleeves and open at the neck to reveal a V of that dark, springy mat of hair Dawn remembered so distinctly from last night. With difficulty, she subdued a flush of shameful memory and returned his cool gaze. If it were to be his policy to ignore what had passed between them, her wisest course was to follow suit.

She said, with forced pleasantness, 'As a matter of fact, it is. But it can't be today. I'd like to get started with all those shots of the castle I missed yesterday.'

'By all means,' he replied in a casual, dismissing tone. 'Make yourself at home.' He turned to Vernon. 'Did you bring the books with you? I'd like to get started on them right away; we're both needed back at the plant.'

Vernon gulped the last of his tea and rose. 'Of course. I'll just set up in the office.'

Dawn was acutely aware of their solitude when he was gone, but she refused to flee Byron's presence like a nervous child. She made herself sit and sip her coffee deliberately, not looking around at him, ignorning him as he was choosing to ignore her. After a time he walked over to the window and looked out. She hastily finished the remainder of her coffee and started to rise.

'I suppose by now you've heard the whole sordid story.' He spoke abruptly, and she looked at him, startled.

'I don't know what you mean.'

He turned, contempt and distaste narrowing in his eyes. 'After what you heard in the garden last night you couldn't wait to pry all the gory little details out of my sister. You women are all alike. You have absolutely no concept of the sanctitude of privacy!'

'For your information,' she flared, 'I haven't even *seen* your sister today! As for all women being alike—that's probably the most narrow-minded, chauvinistic thing I've heard you say since I've been here, which is saying a great deal!'

He withstood her onslaught implacably. 'Then you deny that you know anything at all about my connection with Hilary Mann?'

She looked down at her hands. 'No,' she admitted miserably, 'I don't deny it.'

He uttered a single triumphant, 'Ha!' and she jerked her head up.

'Maggie told me, last night,' she defended hotly, 'and *not* because I asked!'

'I find that very difficult to believe,' he returned coolly. 'I suggest, *Miss* Morrison, that your first item of business here was to discover whether the lord of the castle were married, involved, or——' a hatefully mocking twist of the lips, 'on the rebound.'

Dawn jumped up from the table. 'My first and only item of business,' she told him, controlling her voice with some difficulty, 'was to complete my assignment and be out of your way as quickly as possible. Now, if you'll excuse me . . .' She turned to go, but then remembered. With a breath, she turned back to him, in control now, firmly businesslike. 'One other thing. I'll need your permission to take some shots of the old tapestries and portraits in the original parts of the castle.'

He was glowering into his cup, and did not respond.

'I should tell you,' she continued, feeling faintly superior now in her own realm, 'that repeated exposure to the high-intensity of flash bulbs can sometimes cause a breakdown in the materials of old pigments and dyes. I don't think that needs to be an immediate concern with only a few exposures, but of course it's your decision.'

He replied curtly, without looking up, 'Do as you wish.'

She started again towards the door, and this

time did not turn at the sound of his voice. 'By the way, you'll find your camera bag on your bed. I hope the dew hasn't done it any damage.' His voice changed subtly, faintly taunting. 'Really, Dawn, you must learn not to let your violent emotions sweep away your judgment so. It's a valuable piece of equipment and your livelihood, and after all, your career does come first, doesn't it?'

She stepped through the door and closed it behind her with an unsatisfactory bang. Naturally, he would have the last word.

She spent the day entirely on her own, and the hours flew past until lunchtime. She was not very adventurous in the morning, concentrating on getting the dull part of her job—the meticulous details and pictures of the accommodation—out of the way so that the rest of her stay could be devoted to capturing the glamour and romance of the island on film. She and Maggie lunched alone, for Byron had already finished his business with Vernon and gone to the distillery, and she was not sorry. He was right, she *had* let her emotions momentarily come before her job, and it was a mistake she vowed not to make again.

Maggie offered to take her around, but Dawn declined. She could capture much more of the atmosphere, the charm of the castle, if she were allowed to make her discoveries on her own. Beginning with the tower of her own room, she carefully set up her tripod and various lenses, and spent almost half an hour getting what she hoped was the perfect shot of the tapestry on the wall.

The staircase leading to the exhibition rooms was well marked and brightly lit, and she followed it eagerly. It opened on to a stone chamber which might have been transported intact at the height of its glory directly from the fifteenth century. There was a printed description on the glass-covered pedestal in the doorway, and she scanned over it quickly. 'The Master Chamber of the Lord and his Lady . . .'

And the following words were read out loud over her shoulder, in a masculine voice, 'This room was used for much more than sleeping . . .' She turned to look at Byron and he favoured her with another one of his provocative lifts of the brow. 'But then so are a great many bedrooms around the world.' She stepped deliberately away from him and into the room, focusing her camera on the great dais bed in the centre piled high with its many fur rugs. He continued to read, 'It was the centre of activity for family life. Here the lady would sew and tend her children while the lord often conducted business or entertained guests. Dining was done here as well on occasion, and it was not unusual for the couple to take five or six of their favourite hounds to bed with them for warmth.' Again, he inserted a wry opinion. 'I'm certain I could have thought of a better arrangement than *that*!'

Dawn snapped the shutter and changed lenses to get a wide view of the throne chair and the fireplace on the opposite side of the room.

'Sleeping arrangements were very crude. The mattress was usually no more than corn shucks or straw covered with animal skins, and when the ticking became soiled or lost its resilience it was merely scattered along the floor to absorb odours and animal droppings. The lord and lady always slept nude.'

She turned to glare at him. 'That wasn't written there.'

'No,' he followed her into the room. 'But you seem to me a woman with an inquisitive mind, and I thought you might like to be enlightened on the subject. Maggie sent me up to check on you. She thought you might be lost.'

'As you can see,' she returned, busy with her camera, 'I'm not.'

She took a few more shots about the room, but suddenly the glamour was dimmed for her. Despite its present soft allure of polished wood and brass-studded chests, colourful carpets and plush furs, Byron's description had filled the ancient chamber with the vision of flea-bitten, snapping hounds and the odour of dung, and her romantic concept of medieval life would never be the same. She thought he had done it on purpose.

She moved her equipment into the next room, small and almost spartan in its furnishings, and Byron announced, 'The maiden's chamber. Now, she *never* slept nude. To have been discovered doing so would probably have meant dismemberment for the gallant knight who was commissioned to sleep outside her door, guarding the sacred vessel. A virgin daughter was a possession beyond jewels in those days, you know. Fortunately, customs have changed, or else most of the fathers of the world today would be paupers.'

Dawn kept her mind on her work and a sharp rein on her tongue. Was Byron's penchant for denigrating women a reflection of his opinion of the sex in general, or a blow aimed exclusively at her? She suspected his main motive at this moment was to trap her into another flare of temper, and she refused to succumb.

'Often,' he continued airily, 'the most barbaric methods were used to protect that treasure. The chastity belt, for example, is thought to be the precursor of the dreadful blight of venereal disease that afflicts the world to this day. Have you ever seen one? Beastly-looking things.'

She turned on him. 'Why do you do this?' she demanded with as much calm and impartiality as she could muster.

He looked innocent. 'Do what?'

'Insist upon turning everything romantic into something shameful and—dirty! Chop away at women as though we were each personally responsible for Eve's fall from grace. Turning femininity into something cheap and—tasteless!'

The unruffled lift of his eyebrow told her that she had stepped directly into his trap. '*I* do that, Miss Morrison? It seems to be that it's you who holds femininity in distaste. The eternal business person too preoccupied with making a place for herself in a man's world to allow herself to be a woman—as though your gender were something you're ashamed of.'

Her temper flared, but she struggled to keep it from showing. 'I have just as much right to make a place for myself in the world as any man,' she told him shortly. 'And it would be a lot easier if I didn't have to constantly fight off men like you who think women were designed for only one thing. I resent your attitude, Mr Boyd,' added coldly. 'Just because you've been disappointed by one woman it's no excuse for turning your bitterness towards the entire feminine sex.' Because the venom behind her words was beginning to show, she turned deliberately back to her camera. 'I think you do belong in the Middle Ages. I understand men back then disliked women too.'

After a moment she heard the purposeful click

of his footsteps moving away from her, and she suddenly felt very tired.

Byron was absent from the dinner table, this time, Maggie explained, owing to the last-minute malfunction of machinery at the distillery, and once again they had a cosy meal alone. Maggie told her that she had timed her visit perfectly, to coincide with the gala celebration of Spring Fest in the native tradition which would take place towards the end of her stay.

'It's really an exciting thing to see,' she said. 'The castle courtyard is opened up and everyone comes in native dress at sunset bearing torches and chanting the ancient Gaelic planting song. All the cooking is done outside, and everyone lies back on cushions and pallets and eats and drinks and dances until dawn. The revelry on the lawn will take you right back to the fifteenth century.'

Dawn agreed that it was something she would not want to miss, and thought that would make a nice addition to her article.

She went to bed dreaming of the coming festival, the colourful costumes, the beating drums, the wildly whirling torches, and it seemed she could almost hear the music ... She was dragged out of slumber by that persistent melody and lay there in the darkness for a time, gradually realising it was not a dream.

In fact, it could hardly be referred to as a melody, but more of a chant, toneless and high-pitched, augmented occasionally by the minor chords of guitar. It had a strange beauty of its own, eerie, wild, and oddly sensuous. She got out of bed and switched on a low lamp, crossing the room to fling open the casement window. The night air was chill as she leaned out, vainly searching the garden below for the source of the disturbance, but the music was provocative and she could not go back inside.

Then on a high, vibrant note, it stopped, and there was the faint stir of chords as though the guitar had been set down. It sounded very close.

'Rapunzel, Rapunzel,' came the soft voice below her, 'let down your hair.'

Dawn started at the familiar voice and words and leaned further out, searching the darkness. 'Where are you?' she hissed. 'What are you doing?'

'I'm here, below your window.' His voice was conversational now, at a normal speaking tone. And so clear that he could have well been in the room with her. 'As for what I'm doing—merely seeking to disparage your theory of my opinion of women by showing you I don't regard you cheaply. That you're worth, in fact, a romantic serenade beneath your bedroom window in the true Hebridean custom. How do you like our Gaelic music?'

There, she could see it now—the slight protrusion of a portion of a portico directly below her. It must be there that Byron stood, looking up at her, but she could not see either form nor face of him.

She said, 'It's—different. But nice, in a way.'

'Most people don't understand it. Musically, it's off key and unstructured, but if folk music is supposed to epitomise the character of the people it describes, it serves its purpose very well. Islanders are all basically wild and unstructured, a people unto themselves.'

Dawn was aware that he had the advantage, in that he could see her in her low-necked nightgown and flowing hair, but she could not see him. 'Well,' she said, a little uncomfortably, 'thank you for the serenade . . . Goodnight.' She started to pull the window closed, but the sound of his voice stopped her.

'Now that I've made an effort to prove you wrong about what I think of the feminine sex, I should like to put the question to you.'

She hesitated, puzzled. 'What?'

'I suggest that all those ugly opinions you ascribed to me this afternoon could more aptly apply to you. I think you hold your own femininity in contempt.'

She scowled. 'That's ridiculous! And so is this conversation. Goodnight.'

Once again he stopped her. 'Why haven't you married? Surely it's not because no one has asked you.'

The question was an uncomfortable one, and also a little painful. She could not explain to him, arrogant, conceited, and already contemptuous, how the scars of her parents' divorce would never leave her, how they had led her to set impossibly high standards for the man she would marry— standards which included permanence, stability, and unswerving loyalty. How much emotional turmoil she had endured through the years because of men who saw only a pretty face and did not suspect her deeper needs, and how, eventually, she had learned to supply those needs herself by throwing herself completely into her work . . . She said, stiffly, 'I don't think that's any of your business.'

A disembodied voice floating up to her from the dark, he persisted, 'Have you a man waiting back home?'

'No,' she answered shortly, and reached again to pull the window closed.

'Ah, I rest my case.' The soft satisfaction in his voice made her stop. 'You *are* ashamed of your femininity, or afraid of it, so you hide yourself in ugly dresses and unattractive hairstyles and go out into the world to compete with men, rather than enjoy them in a natural relationship.' Now his voice altered subtly, and being unable to see his face was maddening. 'I'll give you one last chance, Rapunzel, love. Let down your hair ...'

Deliberately, Dawn pulled the window shut and got back into bed. She lay there in the darkness for a long time, shivering with cold, her heart racing with anticipation as she heard his footsteps in the hall outside the door, and then slowing again as she heard his own door open and softly close. Still she lay there, hugging herself miserably, because she knew that every word he had spoken tonight had been true.

The next morning she met Byron in the dining room, and he casually invited her to come with him to the distillery. 'If you're going to write about the true nature of the island,' he told her, 'the article wouldn't be complete without it.'

And so within an hour she climbed into his white Mercedes, her camera on the seat between them, for the ten-minute drive across the asphalt to the distillery. 'I hope you don't have a weak stomach,' said Byron as they pulled through a chain-link gate and into the parking lot of a long, low, rambling building. 'Some of the odours of fermentation can take your breath away if you're not used to them.'

'I'll be all right,' she assured him competently,

and he only glanced at her in amusement as he helped her out of the car.

He took her first to a large, barn-like building whose interior was dark and musty and lined with endless rows of wooden barrels. 'This is our ageing warehouse. We don't sell any whisky under five years old. Some of it's twelve, fifteen, and twenty years old—but of course that's already purchased, and we're merely ageing it for the buyer.' Some men were working along the rows, shifting the barrels and marking on file cards which hung below each one the date and the time. 'It has to be turned at intervals. A lot of companies use machinery for this; we still do it by hand.'

'Wouldn't it be cheaper, in the long run, to install machinery?' Dawn asked.

He glanced at her. 'Perhaps. But it would put a lot of men out of work. We like the old ways.'

The interior of the building was like a dungeon, down a cold, damp flight of stairs, into a huge, crowded, noisily echoing stone chamber lit in the eerily flickering blue-green of fluorescent tubes. Already the faint sour odour of rotting grain reached her, mixed with machine oil and human perspiration, and she busied herself with the light-meter of the camera to try to push the unpleasant sensations aside.

'We'll start at the beginning, shall we?' Byron had to shout over the grinding and clanging of machinery and the other shouts of workers. Now she was grateful for his protective arm on her elbow as he guided her towards another extension of the main chamber.

'Of course the real beginning is out in the fields, with the harvesters. They bring the grain here, where it's washed and sorted for defects, prepared with special enzymes, and mixed with sugar and water for the mash.' She snapped her camera on the dozen or so workers, many of them women, who bent over huge tubs or sat at long tables, their nimble fingers flying through the grain.

He led her to another room filled with vats, each as large as a swimming pool, and the musky, unhealthy odour that prevailed was like a physical thing. 'This is where the mash ferments,' he said, stepping inside and watching her for a reaction. 'The temperature has to be carefully controlled and the entire process checked periodically.'

It was warm and humid, and the vile odour of decay seemed to permeate every step she took, clinging to her hair and her clothes and darting towards the back of her throat. She felt nausea rising and it was difficult to breathe. But she took a few pictures and followed him as he crossed the room to check the temperature gauge.

'Every part of the process is important,' he was saying, 'but this is one of the most crucial.' He glanced at her, then reached into his pocket for his handkerchief. 'Put this over your face,' he suggested gently. 'It will help a little.'

Dawn swallowed hard and shook her head. 'No—thanks. I'm okay, really.'

He slipped his arm about her waist as they walked towards the door. 'A *lady*,' he told her, 'would have at least had the decency to swoon in my arms.' But she thought there was a glint of admiration in his eyes that she had not.

Back out into relatively fresh air again, he paused and tilted his head, listening above the clatter to a P.A. system: 'Mr Boyd ... extension two-one ... Mr Boyd, please.'

'Come on up to the office for a minute,' he said,

his hand on her back lightly guiding her towards another flight of stairs. 'This won't take long.'

The office area was the perfect antithesis to the nether regions of actual distillation: clean and bright and plushly decorated with powder blue carpeting and bright blue and brown wallpaper depicting various labels off the centuries-old Falkone's Whisky bottles. There was a display of these old bottles on one wall of the reception room, and a busy, middle-aged secretary at the desk. Suddenly Dawn was struck by a title for her article: Falkone's Acres, Past and Present—Five Centuries of Scottish History. And she excitedly began to snap pictures of everything in sight.

The secretary looked at her curiously, but spoke to Byron. 'It's London. Mr Clark.'

'I'll take it in my office,' he replied, and just then the door to another office opened and two people emerged.

He was bald and middle-aged, she was tall, slender and strikingly beautiful. She wore a tailored suit whose colour must have been chosen precisely to match the décor of the office, the skirt was slit to reveal a line of shapely calf and knee, a powder-puff fur collar brushed against her thick, gleaming red hair. With a sinking heart, Dawn saw the muscles in Byron's face tighten, and she knew who the girl was.

After a moment he spoke, although apparently with some difficulty. 'Dawn, I don't believe you met Hilary Mann, and her father, Thomas. This is Dawn Morrison, from *Americans Abroad* magazine.'

The other girl nodded at her, though her eyes were glittering strangely, and Thomas Mann stepped forward to take her hand. Byron abruptly excused himself and closed the door to his office.

'Charmed to meet you, Miss Morrison,' said Mr Mann. 'Byron is taking you on a little tour, I see. Is there anything I can do to show you around while he's occupied?'

'Thank you, no,' she replied, trying not to return the stare of the other woman, which was beginning to make her uncomfortable. 'I'll wait for Byron.'

'Very well, then, I do have some work to finish up . . .' He turned to his daughter. 'I'll see you at noon, then, my dear.'

He left them alone, and Dawn turned to face that discomfiting gaze being directed upon her. Hilary's lips were upturned coolly in a smile, as though Dawn had been measured and found wanting. 'Well, well,' she said softly, at last. 'So you're his next victim!'

'I don't understand what you mean,' returned Dawn stiffly.

'You will, my dear,' the other girl drawled. 'You will.'

And just then the door to Byron's office opened.

Ignoring Hilary, he said pleasantly, 'Come in, Dawn, and sit down while I finish up some papers for the morning post. It won't take long, I promise.'

She was so grateful for the rescue that she went gladly.

Byron sat upon the edge of the desk and smiled at her as she took the comfortable leather chair opposite. 'So. What do you think of the operation so far?'

'It's fascinating. It's really going to add something to the article. But I thought you had work to do.'

He lifted his shoulders lightly. 'Not really. You just looked as if you could use an interruption out there. It wasn't very kind of me to leave you in her clutches.'

Dawn answered carefully, 'She is rather— intimidating.'

He stood up and came over to her. 'Let's not talk about her just now.' He bent over and took her shoulders, lifting her gently to her feet. 'I'd rather talk about something I've been wanting to do since I first saw you this morning ... maybe longer than that.'

She could see it in his eyes, very close to hers, but still she had to whisper, 'What's that?'

'Kiss you.'

His lips touched hers lightly, gradually pressing into a tenderness and a warmth she had never known before, and she welcomed him gladly. Her arms slipped around his neck and her fingers caressed the fine material of his worsted suit, her heart was leaping and cascading with unrestrained joy. She admitted for the first time that of all the men she had known, all the times she had been kissed, *he* was the only one by whom she had ever really wanted to be kissed, *he* was the only one by whom she had ever really wanted to be held, and with that admission came a new freedom in the joy of exploring her feelings. She wanted him to never stop.

But of course he must. When he released her and lifted his head she whispered, 'Oh, Byron ...' And then froze at the cold and calculating look in his eyes.

She twisted to the direction of his gaze, and there, watching them through the glass window, a coolly superior smile on her lips, was Hilary. And

Byron had known it all along. He had brought her in here, deliberately arranged her to stand before the window, knowing all along ... Hilary raised her hand in light greeting, then moved out of their range of vision.

Dawn stepped away with no resistance from Byron, a miserable feeling churning in the pit of her stomach.

Once again, she had been royally used.

CHAPTER FIVE

IN the days which followed Dawn completely immersed herself in her work, doing her best to avoid Byron. This was made somewhat easier by the fact that he was spending most of his time at the distillery, in angry telephone conversations with Thomas Mann, or closeted in the office with Vernon, going over accounts. Dawn told herself this was best. She had come dangerously close to becoming involved in a distracting and self-destructive situation which could only shatter her peace of mind if she allowed it to go further. She needed every ounce of concentration she could preserve to complete her assignment, for it would be the best thing she had ever done.

In those days she came to realise she was in love. She loved every nook and cranny of the stalwart, impenetrable fortress. She loved the centuries of proud, aristocratic Boyds who gazed down at her fiercely from the portrait gallery in the upper floor. She loved every winding path and sculpted hedge in the garden, the placid black lake which reflected the foreverness of the castle, through joy and sorrow, victory and defeat, never changing, day after day. She loved the indomitable tradition of loyalty and mastery which was the Boyd heritage, and every shred of that emotion would go into her photographs. It was a labour of love.

She met Vernon in the foyer one morning as she was planning to take a brief excursion around the castle grounds. She had planned to ask Maggie for the use of a car to make a tour of the village and perhaps some of the more scenic areas of the island, but she had already left the house and Dawn decided to make best use of the time by exploring on foot.

'Good morning,' he greeted her cheerfully. 'How's it going?'

'Very well, I think,' she returned. 'I'll be able to wrap it up in not much more than a week.'

'How about sending us a preview copy?'

She laughed. 'That's not really my department, but I'll see what I can do.'

Byron came clattering down the tower staircase just then, his eye on his watch, briefcase in hand. He was dressed in a dark blue suit, jacket unbuttoned to reveal a silk shirt of a lighter blue patterned silk, and the colour, as always, softened his features and made him look much less formidable. His manner of dress was usually much more casual, and Dawn knew before he spoke that he did not intend to spend the day at the plant.

He greeted Vernon abruptly. 'Sorry, old man, but I have to fly to Glasgow this morning. I'll be back later tonight, but that won't give us time to get much work done. Let's have a fresh go at it in the morning, shall we?'

He did not look at Dawn, or even acknowledge her presence. She wondered with a stab of unplanned hurt whether that, too, were part of the tradition of Boyd men. To use women for their own purposes and then cast them aside, forgotten, as soon as they became no longer necessary.

When he had gone Vernon turned to her with an uncertain smile and Dawn quickly masked her own eyes. 'Well,' he said, a little too exuberantly, 'looks as if I'm free for the day. What about you?'

'I'd planned to take some outside shots, a little of local colour, that sort of thing . . .' she began.

'Good.' Gallantly, he scooped the camera bag from her shoulder. 'This is the perfect day for me to take you on a first-class tour of the island.'

Vernon drove an old jeep which had seen its share of unpaved roads and long miles. With the canvas top down it was a little chilly, but it provided an unimpaired view of the surrounding countryside, and Dawn did not have to bother with windows and frames when she asked him to stop for her photographs. They drove through unpaved, wooded paths first towards the range of ragged mountains jutting towards the sky, and Vernon explained, 'This is part of the castle's original game park. The lord of the island had exclusive rights to the hunting here, and anyone caught poaching usually ended up minus a finger or two. Incredible, isn't it, to think some of these trees have been standing since the time of knights and fair damsels? What tales they could tell!'

Dawn agreed that it was, indeed, incredible, and almost forgot her camera as she allowed herself to be transported by the spell of the forest. It was cool and dark beneath the trees, and the smells of rich earth and moss and fragrant flowering shrubs rose on every breeze. She allowed her imagination to run rampant. She could hear the gentle clip-clop of a destrier's hooves on the turf, see rounding the corner a tall knight in plated armour bearing the azure and silver colours of the Boyd standard, and when he lifted his visor the face of the knight was Byron's . . . She smiled a little at her foolishness and turned her attention back to what Vernon was saying.

'Of course you know how Falkone's Acres got its name.'

She shook her head curiously.

'The island used to be a nesting ground for falcons. Back then, a well-trained hunting falcon was very valuable. The first baron used to capture and train them and became very famous for his birds. Unfortunately they've all disappeared, now. Civilisation, I guess.'

Dawn wondered if the real reason Byron objected so to the opening of the island to the public was that he feared his own way of life would go the way of the falcons.

When they emerged from the covering of the trees they noticed that the illusion of darkness had not been due entirely to the forest. The tops of the mountains were swathed in circular clouds and the sky was hazy and grey. 'Oh-oh,' said Vernon. 'Looks as if we might get a shower before the day's out.'

The entire island was less than fifty miles square and could easily be driven around in a day. Dawn marvelled at the vast geographical differences compacted into such a small space, and agreed with Vernon that the possibilities for successful tourism were limitless. 'Byron has been sitting on a goldmine all these years,' he said. 'I've tried to tell him, but ...' He shook his head helplessly and Dawn understood. She thought she was beginning to understand more of Byron every day.

They stopped for lunch of crispy fried fish, and crunchy chips in a little café in the village. They had a window table, and Dawn was delighted by the colourful sights and sounds from the street. Vendors barked their wares from brightly painted handcarts, slim dark girls strolled through the streets in sari-like garments tucked up at the waist and bare feet, a strolling musician passed by, and when he smiled at her it reminded her of Byron.

'I know it's none of my business,' Vernon was saying, and she quickly brought her attention back to him. He looked uncomfortable, staring into his tea cup, and then glancing at her. 'But have you and Byron had some sort of tiff?'

She was startled. 'Why, whatever makes you say that?'

He shrugged, now avoiding her eyes. 'I don't know. As I said, it's none of my business. It's just that he's been so moody and irritable lately, and when your name is mentioned he practically goes through the ceiling. You haven't noticed the way he watches you? I imagine he doesn't mean for you to see. But I've noticed, and—well, I would just hate to think there's some misunderstanding between the two of you that could be patched up.'

'No,' said Dawn, and managed a smile. 'No misunderstanding.' But this she could not comprehend at all. Why should Byron be giving any thought to her, pleasant or unpleasant? She thought surely it was Vernon who had misunderstood.

They walked about the town under the lowering sky, stopped in at a fresh fruit market, bought a pastry from the baker, and Vernon talked about Byron. It was a subject with which Dawn never got bored.

'One nice thing about living on a private island,' he said, gesturing about him. 'There are no parking meters. No traffic courts, either.'

That brought up an interesting question. 'There must be some civil disputes, with so many people living together. Who settles them?'

He smiled. 'Byron does. Very informally, of

course. Nothing he says or does is legally binding except as it applies to his employees, but it's always worked about very well, and no one has questioned his judgment yet. He has such a marvellous way with people.'

This she found hard to believe, and it must have registered on her face.

Vernon said, 'You've got to understand that Byron has been under a lot of pressure lately. This thing with the tourism, and business matters and—personal problems. He hasn't been exactly himself. He's really a wonderful chap, you know. Only an extraordinary person could manage all this the way he does—over a thousand people living and working together and perfectly content with themselves and their lives. He's directly responsible for it all.'

Dawn thought that if Byron were still playing the role of ancient lord of the island, Vernon fitted perfectly into the part of his loyal serf and number one admirer.

It was late in the afternoon when they got back into the car again, and the sky was beginning to look ominous. Vernon, glancing at it with an air of assessment, said, 'I think we have time for a quick drive around the beach, if you like.'

It was the long way back to the castle, and getting a little too murky for the kind of outdoor shot Dawn wanted, but she had nothing pressing her to return to the castle, so she agreed. They drove along a winding coastal road, overlooking at points a sheer drop over the jagged cliffs where the greying sea pounded against the rocks, and Dawn was astonished to notice fishermen wading chest deep into the vicious surf with their lines and poles.

'What are they doing?' she gasped. 'Isn't that dangerous?'

'Not if you know how. Weather like this brings the good fish—mackerel and sea trout—right into the shore. Naturally, fish is a major part of the diet of islanders, so it's worth it.'

The road wound down closer to the beach, where patches of the luscious pink thrift grew wild in the grass and seemed to melt right into the ocean. 'On my first day here,' Dawn remembered, 'I found a patch growing way up in the woods, near the castle. I wondered at it growing so far from the sea.'

'There must have been a salt-water pond or lake there at one time or the other, and it left enough sea minerals in the soil to support ocean vegetation.' Vernon laughed a little. 'The natives will tell you that thrift growing inland marks the gateway to a house of romance and heartbreak. I suppose that description could fit the castle well enough, all things considered over the centuries.'

Dawn shivered in the rising wind and drew her cardigan more closely over her shoulders. She wondered if that, too, had become a tradition of Falkone's Acres.

She was surprised to find on the northern end of the island a barrage of silent bulldozers and cranes surrounding a shallow pit of cleared land large enough to easily accommodate a shopping centre. It was a shock to stumble upon such obvious signs of industrialisation after being immersed all day in the primitive beauty of the island, and Dawn found herself hoping deeply that civilisation had not gone that far.

Vernon laughed at her suggestion about the shopping centre. 'What in the world would we do with something like that? No, I'm afraid those marvellously convenient monstrosities are limited to your part of the world, Dawn. This is going to be the new packing and distributing plant for the distillery. We've outgrown the old one. It's a necessary evil, and besides, it keeps men in jobs.'

That last statement echoed hauntingly of Byron.

It became misty as they drove towards the castle, clinging with clammy dampness to Dawn's face and neck and clouding her eyes. 'Oh dear,' said Vernon. 'We'd better head for shelter pretty quick. The cover on this old rattletrap hasn't worked since I bought it.'

'There's a house,' pointed Dawn. 'Anyone you know?'

Vernon glanced at the large, mansard-roofed structure overlooking the sea, and shook his head. 'That's the Manns' place. I don't think we'd better.'

Dawn was inclined the agree.

After a moment, while the mist became thicker and his driving more cautious, he said, 'I suppose you've heard about the mess with Hilary Mann.'

'Some,' she replied carefully. 'I understand that Byron is trying to buy out of the partnership.'

'It would be a mistake,' he answered, 'but what else can he do?'

'Perhaps,' suggested Dawn, for no other reason than a sudden sharp recurrence of the memory of hurt and abuse she had recently suffered at the hands of Hilary and Byron, 'he could try being a bit more tolerant.'

The gaze he shot at her was pure amazement before he shifted his eyes back to the road. 'Clearly, you haven't heard the whole story. There are certain things a man like Byron can't tolerate in anyone—much less the girl he's going to marry.'

'All I've heard is a lot of one-sided accusations

and half-truths,' she answered. 'There are two
sides to every story.'

'Well, this one is pretty cut and dried. I
personally never could understand what he saw in
Hilary. She's a beautiful woman, true, but so—
manipulative, if you know what I mean. I was
always a little afraid of her. And he put up with
hell from her, too, if you'll pardon the expression,
long before this all came up. It always looked as if
every fight they had would be their last, but she
always got him back. And I'll tell you something
else: I don't think the people of the island would
ever have accepted Hilary as the mistress of
Falkone's Acres.' He spoke as though that were
important. 'Then, one day a couple of months
back, she started making all these trips to the
mainland. Byron never suspected a thing. It turns
out she was chasing after this man in Edinburgh—
one of Byron's biggest competitors, no less. Then
one day she brought him here, and the rest is history.
The rumour now is that she's going to marry the
fellow, and I say good riddance to bad rubbish.'

For some reason, she was disappointed. It
would have made her feel better at that moment to
believe the entire thing had been Byron's fault. It
was wretched to be so hurt by a man and still
understand him. 'So he's afraid that when Hilary
does marry this other man, Falkone's distillery
would be eventually swallowed up by his com-
petitor.'

'That could never happen,' replied Vernon
confidently. 'It would be foolish of them to even
try. Byron will always hold the controlling interest,
and it would even be profitable for another distillery to try to merge. No, it's simply that
honour plays a large part in the Boyds' business

dealings, it always has and it always will. Major
negotiations are sealed with a handshake, and
neither party has ever had to worry that it
wouldn't be binding. He simply refuses to deal
with someone he can't trust.'

Dawn remembered the motto: *Confido*—I trust.
And there was a peculiar yearning in her heart for
a place that treasured so carefully the old ways, a
man who clung so stoically to the old values.

Suddenly it began to rain, great, cold pounding
drops of rain, and they were soaked before Vernon
could stop the car. He gestured to a clump of
rocks and scrubby undergrowth on the hillside.
'Over there!' he shouted, running around to her
side of the car. 'It will at least keep us out of the
downpour!'

He took her hand as he helped her up the
slippery hill, mud sucked at her shoes and one was
completely lost as they scrambled for shelter. He
pushed aside the shrubs this way and that until
they finally found an overhang of rock large
enough to accommodate the two of them. It was
rather cramped, but they squeezed inside, and it
was like a small, dark cave with the steady curtain
of rain forming the door.

'Well,' sighed Vernon, 'that's better. Not much,
but better. These showers usually don't last long. I
would offer you my coat, but it's as wet as your
sweater.'

'It's O.K.,' chattered Dawn, squeezing moisture
out of the hem of her sweater. 'I'm just glad we
found this place. That rain is freezing!'

He smiled at her in the uncertain light, then said
unexpectedly, 'You're not married, are you?'

She was a little taken aback, possibly because it
was the second time in a week she had been asked

that question, and by two strikingly different men. She answered, 'No, I'm not,' and hoped he would not pursue.

'I didn't think so. I mean, I can't imagine a man who would allow his wife to run around the world taking pictures . . . but then American customs are so different from ours.'

She stared at him. 'Any man *I* would marry,' she told him, 'would allow me to do whatever was necessary to pursue my career. Marriage is a partnership, not an enslavement!'

He chuckled. 'I told you your customs were different.'

'I don't see that at all,' she insisted. 'Half the workers at the distillery are women, and you can't tell me all of them are unmarried.'

'No,' he admitted. 'Maybe I was interjecting more of a personal opinion than a true social statement.'

'If Hilary had married Byron,' she added, 'she would have continued to work. If and when I marry I expect the same sort of arrangement.' She was aware that she had spoken her thoughts out loud, and was a little embarrassed because it made it sound as if she associated Hilary's relationship with Byron with her own situation. But she was also a little surprised to discover that, when viewed in that context, her desire for a career took an immediate back seat to the imagined contentments of a home and children. Hadn't Byron summed it up pretty accurately . . . that her violent devotion to her career was simply a substitution for a permanent relationship in her life? And perhaps, when that ultimate, totally perfect man came along with his promises of foreverness and devotion, everything would change . . .

Vernon said abruptly, 'You're in love with him, aren't you?'

Dawn swallowed hard and did not answer. It was not that she refused to, but that she couldn't. She was remembering with a tightening of her throat the cold, vengeful look in Byron's eyes as he turned to Hilary after having kissed her, and her own pulmetting despair as she realised his display of tenderness towards her was in fact no more than a slap in the face to Hilary. If only, she thought wistfully, that moment could have been as genuine for him as it was for me . . . But she refused to pursue it, not even to herself.

Vernon, watching the changing emotions soften her rain-streaked face, nodded and said nothing. They both turned to stare back at the curtain of rain and the churning surf, and time ticked by in silence.

As Vernon had predicted, the shower did not last long, but it was intense, and when it finally lightened enough to go back to the car they found an inch of water in the floorboard. 'Oh, your poor car!' cried Dawn, but he shrugged it off.

'She's been through worse than this,' he assured her, and tried the key. It ground and choked out. Dawn looked at him sympathetically, and he tried again, to no avail.

'It's too far to walk back,' he apologised wretchedly. 'Especially——' He glanced at her one remaining waterlogged shoe clutched in her hand. 'Barefoot! Oh dear, Dawn, I'm awfully sorry about this.'

'The rain wasn't your fault!' she insisted. 'Come

on, do whatever it is you do under the hood and I'll try the key.'

It took over an hour before they heard the longed-for sound of the motor catching and accelerating. Jubilantly, they started up the dirt trail which would join with the road to the castle. It was already getting dark, and Dawn suspected she would be late for dinner, but after all, she really did not have to account to anyone at the castle. She was only sorry to have put Maggie out, and possibly worried her.

They had gone perhaps a mile before they bogged down in mud. Vernon apologised profusely all the time he was pushing and rocking and trying to dig the back tyres out of the mud, and Dawn felt so sorry for him she went out of her way to be philosophical. 'Don't be silly,' she told him when they were finally on their way again. 'It's been a real adventure!' She tried to ignore the fact that she was wet and muddy and chilled to the bone; it was past nine o'clock and she was starving.

At last the warm yellow lights of the castle came into view, shining like a beacon through the fog and darkness, and Dawn could not remember ever having been so glad to come home. A moment later she had to remind herself this was not her home, after all, and wonder why she should think of it as such.

Vernon pulled up before the front steps. 'I won't come in,' he said, 'I'm a mess. Dawn, I can't tell you how sorry I am . . . you've been a real sport about it.'

'Honestly,' she assured him, 'it's nothing to get upset about. I had a great time today and got some terrific shots, and the rain couldn't be helped.'

'I hope your camera isn't damaged,' he offered miserably.

'Oh, no, the bag is insulated and I kept it pretty dry under my sweater.'

And because he just sat there, gripping the steering wheel, looking like a half-drowned, scolded puppy, she leaned forward and gave him a light peck on the cheek. 'Thanks for a wonderful day,' she said, and smiled. 'I mean it.'

After a moment, Vernon returned her smile, and she got out of the car. As he drove away she turned and started up the steps. And there, outlined against the light of the door, looking like a feudal warrior greeting the enemy, was Byron.

Dawn climbed the steps silently, aware as each step drew her closer of his ominous stance, the hard, angry lines of his face. At last, when she stood directly below him, he spoke. 'Where have you been?' he demanded.

'Vernon drove me around the island,' she explained a little hesitantly. 'We got caught in the rain and then the car wouldn't start . . .'

He turned on his heel and stalked back inside. Confused, she followed him. 'I'm sorry if I upset anyone . . . I didn't plan to be gone so long . . .'

In the foyer, he whirled on her. 'I'll just bet you didn't!' he spat. 'We've been half out of our minds with worry while you're off in the woods somewhere with—Vernon! Well, I hope you enjoyed it!'

'Enjoyed . . .' She stared at him, aghast. 'Now, just wait a minute! I told you what happened . . . though why it should be any concern of yours I'm sure I didn't know——'

'That's right,' he said, his anger working itself into a cold flame. 'It is none of my business.' His eyes raked her up and down, from her half-loose, wet hair tangled with bits of leaves and mud, to the satin shirt which was plastered to her body beneath the sweater so revealingly it need not have been there at all, to the bare feet, and Dawn felt herself begin to burn with his insinuation. 'Go upstairs,' he said icily, 'and put some clothes on.'

Her reserve shattered, and she flung the camera bag on to a nearby throne chair with a force that completely disregarded the expensive lenses and delicate adjustments of the instrument. 'I am *not* one of your—serfs! You have no right to talk to me that way, to imply—what you're implying! Even if it were true—which it most certainly is not!—what gives you the right to censure my behaviour? You may think you own everyone else on this island, body and soul, but you have no hold over me—none whatsoever!'

'That,' he replied with a barely-maintained evenness to his own tone, 'is apparent. I may not have any 'hold' over you, my dear, but I do claim a certain amount of control over what goes on under my roof, and I will not have a guest in my house attempting to seduce one of my employees!'

Dawn gasped, and was speechless.

'Oh, yes,' he taunted her. 'And you don't try very hard to hide the fact, do you? You come in here, looking like a wanton, half dressed——'

She interrupted, incredulously, 'My shoe——'

'And did you think I wouldn't see you kiss him right there on the front lawn?'

'A freindly kiss on the cheek——!'

Byron laughed bitterly, shaking his head with a sharp jerk. 'You almost had me fooled for a while, I'll admit that! I suspected what you were from the first—any woman with looks like yours can only be after one thing. Romance and adventure in the Scottish Isles, right? A two-week roller-coaster of passion, another conquest to take back to the States with you and brag about to your girl friends. You tried it with me, but it didn't work, so you turned to the first available man for a substitute. Poor old Vernon, he's not much of a catch, at that, but any port in a storm, as they say, eh?'

She cried, incredulous and furious, 'How—dare you—accuse *me*——'

'Yes,' he shot back, his eyes black with snapping wrath, 'I dare! I told you before, Dawn, I'm sick of women who make promises they don't keep, so if you think for one moment you'll be welcome in my house after tonight——'

'Promises?' she objected shrilly. 'What promises? What are you talking about?'

'Of course,' he returned sardonically, 'it would mean nothing to you. A few kisses on the sly, a come-hither look, a provocative nightgown ... every one of them a promise of something more, and every one of them a lie.'

Dawn drew a shaky breath. This was incredible, she could hardly believe it was happening, but her own angry instinct for self-defence came to the surface. 'I—promised *you*? You're the one who made the promises, Byron, and you're the one who broke them! Before I even knew you you grabbed me in the woods and forced yourself on me——'

'I've never forced any woman!'

'And what was it to you?' she continued over him, in a high voice. 'A joke—a game! You're the one who tried to make love to me in the garden ... you *knew* my being there was perfectly innocent! And what was that? Just another form of anger.

And the other day—in the office——' She almost
choked on hot tears. 'Every time you've touched
me, Byron Boyd, you've made promises—of
affection, of caring—promises you had no inten-
tion of keeping. When a girl is kissed she likes to
believe it's for some better reason than just getting
even with another woman!'

He stared at her. 'What are you talking about?'
he demanded.

'Hilary!' she returned, blinking back the angry
tears. 'You've been using me ever since I came
here to—get over her—get back at her—to prove
to her, or yourself—oh, I don't know what! But I
do know I don't like it, and if this is a sample of
your—proud honour!—then that . . .' she gestured
behind her to the crest with its mockingly
gleaming motto, 'is a joke!'

'I don't know,' he said in a low voice, 'what
you're talking about.'

'Oh,' she cried airily, her voice becoming hoarse
with the effects of the cold and forcefully repressed
tears. 'I'm sure you don't! I'm also sure that when
you took me into your office the other day you
were totally unaware that Hilary was just outside
the door, and when you kissed me it never crossed
your mind that she had a ringside seat for the
whole event!'

His eyes narrowed ominously. 'You think,' he
said hardly, 'that I arranged that on purpose!'

'That is precisely what I think!' she shot back,
gulping. 'So I suggest before you start throwing
your wild accusations at me you examine your
own closets for skeletons, because I'm tired of
being used!'

She could not stand there a moment longer,
looking at his surprised, angry face, so she turned

and ran up the stairs. Halfway up, she thought she heard Byron call her name, but she did not turn back, because by then the tears had started to flow down her face and she would not have him see her cry.

CHAPTER SIX

ONE phrase above all others kept Dawn awake through the night. '. . . don't imagine you'll be welcome in my house . . .' She tossed and turned and tried to blot the hateful words out of her ears. What had she done to deserve that? Nothing . . . nothing! Only Byron's stupid pride and a misplaced sense of autocracy. She had done nothing to help the matter with her loss of temper in retaliation, and after the things they had said to one another she did not know how she could bear to stay here another hour, and risk facing him again. She only knew that she could not bear to leave, not like this, with him hating her for the lowest kind of woman, and with the despicable accusations she had flung at him still ringing in her ears.

Besides, she rationalised to herself, the article was not nearly finished and she simply could not go back to New York and face her editor with failure on her hands.

She dressed quickly the next morning and waited until she heard his door open, then stepped swiftly out into the hall. He was apparently on his way to the shower; he wearing a short blue velour kimono and apparently nothing else. He carried a razor in one hand and a towel flung over his arm, and his expression as he looked at Dawn was at first nothing more than sleepy surprise. The combination of naked thighs and half-uncovered chest was intimidating, yet at the same time his rumpled hair and stubble of beard was endearing, so that her heart began to pound uncomfortably and she felt herself beginning to blush. Then the expression on his face changed to wry amusement, he leaned back against the door and crossed his arms, letting the kimono part a little more revealingly, and waited for her to speak.

She took a breath, forcefully moving her eyes from the intriguing triangle of crisp hair at his chest to the lazily mocking eyes. She said, 'My work isn't finished yet. I know you would like me to leave, but I can't leave a job half done. It's true that I need the article, but you also need the publicity. If you would only stop and think about it you'd realise how foolish it would be—after all the expense you've gone to, to turn down this opportunity for promotion . . . It might make the difference between profit and loss for you. So,' she smoothed her clammy palms on denim-covered thighs and took another breath, 'if I've offended you I'm sorry, and you can call my editor and complain if you want to. But I'm not walking out on this job without a direct order from him.'

For a time he only looked at her, his cool expression not changing, and the silence was excruciating. Then he said, casually, 'That seems fair enough.' He straightened up and draped the towel over one shoulder. 'Perhaps it's best—for our *professional* relationship—if we forget the unfortunate personal matters which have passed between us.' He started to walk away, then turned back to her with an obeisant inclination of his head. 'Do you mind if I have my shower now, or—was there something else?'

'No,' she said a little shakily. 'That was all.' And she went quickly back into her room.

A reprieve. A few more days to work as quickly and unobtrusively as possible, a few more days to be here, sharing, however peripherally, in the essence of all that was Byron. Arrogant, remote, enigmatic, infuriating, it was all true. Yet possessing the power to send her heart into cascades and spirals whenever he was near, to reduce her to quivering femininity with a single one of his dark, penetrating gazes, to make her forget about her work and her own self-image and all those dearly-held values she had set up for herself over the years with no more than a few well-chosen, drawling words. It was maddening, it was unpardonable, it was positively perverse, the hold he had over her. She knew it would come to nothing and soon she must deal with the fact. She knew that in staying she was only subjecting herself to further hurt and humiliation and would never be more than a passing amusement to Byron, a faint memory to take out over glasses of Scotch whisky with his friends—'the spring that American photographer was here'. Perhaps one day she would come to view this interlude in the same fashion . . . 'my assignment in Scotland . . .' 'the spring I spent in the Hebrides . . .' But never would she recall it with Byron's smooth sophistication. Always there would be wistfulness in her tone, pain in her eyes, and perhaps she would never be able to speak of it at all . . .

Only a few more days. That was all she could ask.

She breakfasted alone, then went to the foyer to retrieve her camera. It was still there, as she had left it, and she flushed at the emotion which had allowed her, once more, to leave a valuable piece of equipment and her livelihood lying around all night, unguarded, forgotten. There were six or seven people milling about farther along the corridor, and Maggie, who was standing among them, talking, raised her hand to Dawn and beckoned her over.

'You might be interested in this,' she said. 'It's court day. Every Saturday,' she explained, 'until noon, Byron holds what the islanders still refer to as "Council"—a direct descendant, believe it or not, of the old feudal custom of the lord of the castle's legal jurisdiction over his fief.' She took Dawn's arm and began leading her towards the office. 'Of course what we have today is a very simple variation, but I do believe you won't find anything else like it in this part of the world. What it boils down to, mostly, is just giving advice—a great many islanders can't read English, you know—but it's the gesture that counts. One of the traditions we simply won't part with. I'm sure Byron wouldn't mind if you watched for a little while if you'd like.'

'Very much,' agreed Dawn. This was what Vernon had told her about yesterday, but she had not imagined so much ceremony was involved. It was a part of island life she simply could not miss.

When they entered the spacious, dark wood and leather office, Byron was sitting behind his desk, leaning over it to speak in soft, rapid Gaelic to the supplicant in dusty corduroys and scuffed boots who sat before it, twisting a battered hat in his hand. He did not glance up at them, but continued speaking until slowly, watching the expression on the other man's face, he smiled, spoke a few more unintelligible words which appeared to conclude the conversation, and the man stood up, bowing and murmuring his thanks.

'Do you mind if Dawn watches for a while?'

enquired Maggie. 'I'm certain she's never seen anything like it.'

Byron leaned back in his chair, regarding her impersonally, through lazy, half-closed eyes. 'No, of course not.' He gestured her to be seated on the far side of the room. 'No pictures, please, and no interruptions. These people expect what goes on in this room to be confidential.'

'Of course,' replied Dawn, a little insulted, and took her seat.

'That last man,' he explained, as Maggie left the room, 'wanted to buy his neighbour's horse, and he wasn't sure he was getting a fair price. I quoted him a price, with which, fortunately, he seemed to agree, so that's one problem solved.'

The next couple who came bursting through the door were middle-aged, married, and in a bad temper. 'I want a divorce,' declared the man before the door was even closed behind him.

Byron looked up in what Dawn suspected was exaggerated astonishment. 'Why, Donald Burns, whatever for?'

'*This* is what for!' He whipped off his hat to reveal a tiny square of plaster on the side of his head. 'I'll tell ye, Mr Boyd, I've had about as much as I can take from this woman! I don't no sooner set foot in the door but she wallops me on the head with a wooden spoon—and for no good reason!'

'I'll give ye reason!' interjected the woman shrilly. 'Sneaking in the house in the dead of night falling down drunk, that's good reason! And after twenty-four years and four children if divorce suits you it never sounded finer to me! No, indeed, it never sounded finer!'

Byron sat back, shaking his head sadly.

'Matilda, Matilda, what am I going to do with you? Now I've told you before you can't go taking a wooden spoon to Donald every time you get angry—one day you're going to hurt him, and how will you feel then? And you,' he turned to the man, 'how would you like it if I gave Jenkins orders not to sell you any more whisky—not a dram?'

'Won't make no difference,' the man muttered. 'I want a divorce.'

'And that just suits me, it surely does!' reiterated the woman.

With a loud sigh, Byron made a note on a pad before him. 'All right. If that's what you want, I'll have to send to the mainland for a magistrate. It will take two or three months.'

'I'll wait,' replied the man with satisfaction, and stalked out of the room. Without a backward glance, his wife followed him.

Byron watched them go, smiling. 'They'll be like two newlyweds before sundown,' he said. 'It's the same thing every month—poor old Donald can't take the stuff, you know; about once a month he has a cup and it goes right to his head. Matilda gets angry and the next morning they're right here, talking divorce. Actually we have very few divorces here.' He chuckled a little. 'Perhaps because it's so inconvenient!'

Dawn had to speak up. 'Perhaps it's better, if two people are that unhappy, to be divorced, than to stay together—for convenience.'

'Donald and Matilda aren't unhappy!' he objected incredulously. 'They just deal with their problems in an unusual way. If coming here to me, and acting out their fantasy of divorce, making threats and letting off steam, helps them keep their marriage together, then there's nothing wrong with that. Marriage is held very sacred here, Dawn. A lot of thought is given to it before a couple marry, and a lot of work goes into it afterwards. I think that may be what's wrong with the family structure in your part of the world—-people just aren't willing to think about it beforehand, or work at it afterwards.'

'Maybe they just don't know about honour,' she volunteered, and when he looked at her in surprise and enquiry, she explained, 'Keeping promises.'

She thought his expression changed slightly as he looked at her, as though he were seeing her for the first time, and what he saw pleased him. It pleased Dawn, too, more than she wanted to admit.

Then he said softly, 'Is that what it is with you, Dawn? Afraid to make the commitment?'

'Maybe,' she responded carefully, 'like you, I simply chose to give it a lot of thought.'

Byron shook his head, rejecting that. 'Choice implies trial and error. You're afraid to make an error, afraid to trust anyone enough to give it a chance.'

She did not understand why, after his remarks that morning, he was once again attempting to get personal with her. She did not particularly like the turn of the conversation, she felt, in fact, that she was stepping on dangerous ground, but there was something in his eyes as he looked at her which warned her, inviting confidence. Perhaps it was no more than he gave to anyone else who came into this room seeking to unburden their problems on to his broad shoulders, but she grasped it like a drowning man clutching at straws. She admitted, 'That may be true—to an extent. My parents were divorced when I was in my teens and I just—never wanted that to happen to me. Maybe I am a little over-cautious because of it. I don't mean to be, but I can't help it.'

The look in his eyes was sympathetic, and it made her heart swell to overflowing with gratitude and—love. He said, 'Let me tell you something, Dawn, that's been handed down in my family for generations. It has to do with our motto—I trust. Because, you see, the secret of obtaining loyalty from another is in being able to first give your trust. It's a two-way street.'

The door opened to admit another petitioner, and suddenly the moment was gone. 'And that little piece of advice,' Byron told her lightly, turning already to the next business at hand, 'comes to you with absolutely no charge whatsoever. Compliments of the house.'

Dawn spent the rest of the day practically sailing through her scheduled tasks, laughing at lunch with Byron and Maggie over some of the petty quarrels which had been solved that morning in his office, feeling ridiculously high-spirited and content. And it was all because Byron was no longer angry with her.

She tried to remember whether she had ever felt this way about a man before. Men were competitors, they were employers, they were predators, and she acted a different role for each of them. No, there had not been, in her adult life, a man whose opinion of her mattered that deeply, who could send her into the deepest of depression with a scowl, or ecstasy with a smile. There had never been a man whose approval she cared to win, or whose very presence could make her hot with anticipation and at the same time cold with dread, who made her long for nearness, desperate for more, and desolate at the thought of separation. Such dependency frightened her as it thrilled her, for never before had she allowed herself to become a victim of her emotions. And she must be careful, she told herself throughout that swift, busy day, very careful . . .

It began to rain late in the afternoon, and continued in a steady downpour which flowed in an unbroken stream down the windows throughout dinner. 'This is typical springtime weather,' Byron told her. 'It was just a streak of odd luck that your first week here was so clear. I hope you've got all the outdoor shots you needed.'

'Not entirely,' she answered. She did not in any way want to bring up the excursion with Vernon which had precipitated such violence between them, so she carefully skirted the subject. 'I thought some shots of your new construction site would be a nice touch . . . progress side by side with antiquity.'

He nodded. 'Maybe we'll have a clear morning before you leave.'

Before she left . . . not even a week from now. She must leave, it was true. She was only a temporary fixture around here, she had a job and friends and an entirely separate life back in New York. *It wasn't for ever*. But she knew that when she did leave a part of her, a very important part, would remain behind.

The dessert was that creamy confection of sponge cake and cream and fruit that the English call trifle, laced extravagantly with sherry. It was delicious, and they lingered over it, Byron and Maggie chatting in a desultory fashion, Dawn sitting back and absorbing all of it lovingly.

Then Byron, pushing away his dish, leaned forward and took one of the candles from the centrepiece. 'Come along, Dawn, this is the perfect night for the tour I promised you.'

'Tour?' She had almost forgotten.

'Certainly.' He stood and extended his hand to her. 'Not afraid of a few ghosts, are you?'

No, she thought as she followed him out of the room. That's not what I'm afraid of.

'Do you really have ghosts?' she chatted as they went into the office to retrieve his keys. She felt it necessary to keep up the light stream of conversation begun at dinner. 'Because that would really add impact to the article, you know. You couldn't keep the tourists away if they thought there was a chance of catching a glimpse of a real, live ghost!'

He looked at her oddly as he took the keys from his desk, and she thought she had said the wrong thing. But he only replied lightly, 'Ghosts are seldom "real" or "live". But yes, we do have one or two, just for appearances' sake. What castle would be complete without them?'

But as they started up the hall he added in a slightly different tone, 'I thought that perhaps now, having got to know us better, you might have wavered a little in your enthusiasm for opening the island to tourism.'

Dawn hesitated. 'In a way,' she said at last, 'I think I almost have. I understand so much better what you're trying to protect, and that it's worth protecting. But then . . .' her voice softened, became almost shy, 'I think of what *I* would have missed if you'd kept the island private, and it doesn't seem fair to deprive others of the same experience. Yes, I still think you're doing the right thing.'

They had reached a doorway, and as Byron paused to insert the key, he stopped and smiled down at her. 'Do you know, I think you've almost convinced me, too.'

He opened the door and ushered her up the narrow stairway ahead of him. It was damp and musty, smelling of a cupboard seldom opened, and his voice echoed and re-echoed as he warned, 'Watch your step now.' His hand was steady and supportive on her back, the candle he held high overhead cast a dim, wavering circle of light over the next step. 'Put your hand out to the right.' She did, and felt a sturdy, rough wooden rail. Byron moved the candle to illuminate the rail which appeared to be no more than the trunk of a slim tree, and beside it a stone wall scarred with time. 'This is it—the stairway where the battle took place. It should be right about here . . . Yes, there it is.' He lowered the candle to reveal a long, deep gash in the wood, and another a little above it.

He bent close over her as he examined the ancient scars of long-ago violence and valour, and the warmth of his body seemed to offer a physical protection against the damp chill rising from the stones. His breath smelled faintly of the wine they had had for dinner and other, less distinct, exclusively masculine scents—his cologne, the wool of his suit, his freshly-laundered shirt—all overwhelming in their subtlety, all wonderfully reassuring and at the same time exciting in that that spoke of his nearness. 'I don't know,' he continued, in a softer tone, as though they were conspirators discovering a secret, 'whether he was trying to dislodge the railing—it's a sheer drop below, you know—or whether this is where the mortal blow was struck.' He moved the candle now to point to the steps below, and in the uncertain light irregular, dark stains were visible, melded into the stone. 'Legend has it that those stains were made by the blood of the enemy.' Dawn shuddered slightly, and he added in a more normal tone, 'I think it's more likely they were made by weather.'

Suddenly there was a bang, reverberating like an explosion through the confined space, a swift draught of wind, and the candle went out. Dawn cried out and clutched for him in the blackness, immediately she felt his strong arms go around her, protecting her, comforting her as one would a small child. And when he spoke there was a note of amusement in his tone, although it was gentle. 'Only the door. The draught blew it closed. Hold on a minute; let me find a match.' He hesitated, one arm still holding her close, and enquired so that she could almost see the teasing gleam in his eyes, 'Unless you'd rather I didn't? I don't mind the dark, if you don't.'

Forcefully, she pushed away, reaching for the rail. 'No,' she said a little unsteadily, 'I'd prefer the candle.'

It seemed like hours that Byron fumbled with the match, and once she reached out and touched his coat, just to assure herself of his presence. She was surprised to feel in return the gentle pressure of his own hand briefly on hers before he moved it away to strike the match. When the chamber flared and dimmed into welcome light again, he was smiling. 'Better?' Then, 'You're shaking!'

'It's—a little cold,' she offered, for she would not for the world admit to him she had been frightened, and, in truth, the dampness was beginning to penetrate her silk shirt and the slim skirt open at the knee.

He quickly shrugged out of his own jacket and draped it over her shoulders. 'I forget. You Americans aren't accustomed to our northern hemisphere temperatures. It can't be below fifty in here; that's warm!' He looked at her, the devasting, teasing glitter back in his eyes. 'Now, how's your sense of adventure? Ready to turn back?'

'Of course not,' she insisted proudly, starting up the stairs. 'I'm still waiting for your ghost!'

'Then I'll take you to him straight away.'

Emerging on to another floor, they walked down a narrow winding hall, cautiously, for the candle did little to penetrate the stuffy blackness, and even their footsteps were muffled. 'You can't even hear the rain up here,' Dawn whispered.

'The walls are six feet thick all around, stronger, in places. And there are no windows. Fresh air was considered bad for the health in those days—not to mention the vulnerability to attack an open window offered. Here we are.' They paused before another scarred wooden door, and it creaked dramatically as Byron opened it with his key.

He swung the candle over head to reveal a small, empty chamber, stone from floor to ceiling, with not even a fireplace to break the monotony. It looked like a prison cell.

'That's exactly what it is, in a manner,' Byron answered her observation. 'There's a Gaelic folk song written about Elspeth and Grant. He was the youngest son of the baron; she was a village maiden. He lost his heart to her; she betrayed him with a local boy. He locked himself in this room— who knows for how long, years, maybe—and grieved himself to death. Some say you can hear his footsteps from the room below, pacing up and down, to this day. And on nights such as this,' his voice lowered to a dramatic whisper, 'when the wind howls and the rain lashes against the castle walls, you can hear his voice, if you listen carefully . . . crying with the torment of the damned for his Elspeth.'

Dawn shuddered again, and he laughed, placing his hand once again on her elbow. 'Come along, I think our Grant has much better taste than to interrupt us on our tour!'

He led her down the corridor through another locked door—this one surprisingly spacious and tastefully decorated with Victorian furnishings. There was a four-postered, canopied bed, embroidered rugs, velvet chaise-longues, claw-footed tables and bureaux that showed no sign of dust in the candlelight. 'This was my grandparents' room,' Byron explained, allowing the door to swing closed behind them and setting the candle on the table beside the bed. 'We still keep it cleaned and dusted, though lord knows why. I expect because so many generations of Boyds were conceived, born, and died here.'

'Why . . . it's very nice.' Dawn went over to the bed and lightly touched the popcorn knit counterpane. 'I don't know why you want to keep it locked up. It's a charming example of almost-contemporary castle life.'

'We have to reserve some right to privacy, don't we?'

He had stepped close to her while she examined the intricate work in the crisp white bedcover, and now as she looked up to respond to his question she felt his arms slip about her, found his face very close to hers, and there was no mistaking the intent in his eyes. Though her senses rose to meet it gladly, with a trembling of her limbs and a pounding of her heart, she placed one hand against his chest, half in protest, half in question, searching his eyes for an answer she did not really expect to find. 'Byron . . .'

'Hush,' he whispered, and he was kissing her.

There was no denying the sensations that made her go weak in his arms, no fighting the response which rose from some sensuous core deep within her and would not be quelled until she was pressing him close, grasping at his shoulders, stroking his hair, opening her mouth to his and still yearning for more.

His fingers had unloosed the pins which bound up her hair, and now it tumbled over her shoulders and down her back, wild in its freedom, yielding to his touch as every other part of her was eager to do. Reverently, Byron lifted a strand, his fingers maddeningly light against the silk which covered her breast, and lifted it to his lips. 'Beautiful hair,' he murmured huskily, kissing it. 'Bedroom hair. Always wear it this way for me, my maddening, irresistible little sylph ... My fairy princess ... You've caught me in your spell and I'll never be free of you ... never ...'

His lips came down on hers again, and she, too, was caught in the spell. The candlelight and the majestic room whirled and receded around her, and it was with no resistance or surprise that she felt herself being lowered gently to the bed.

Then his face was above hers, his lips occasionally sweeping to brush her eyelid or her cheeks or the tip of her nose, his fingers patiently and swiftly working the buttons of her blouse. Her breath was coming with difficulty, her throat was clogged with the pounding of her heart, and every point of her was on fire, but she grasped his hand weakly. 'No, Byron . . .' she whispered. 'What are you doing?'

'I'm going to make love to you,' he answered her softly, and kissed her lips lightly. 'For this one night, Dawn, you're going to learn to trust enough to give yourself completely . . .'

'Please, don't . . .'

The blouse was undone, and he pushed it back gently from her shoulders, gazing for a moment in silent adoration at her in the candlelight. 'Darling,' he whispered, 'you're beautiful.' He bent down to kiss one breast lightly, and she shivered with the sensation and the pain of mounting desire which pulled against her own instincts for self-preservation, too long ingrained to be subdued now. Then he placed his hand beneath her left breast, firm against the rapid, intense vibrations of her heart, and insisted, 'Tell me the truth, Dawn. Tell me you don't want me.'

She almost sobbed. Every fibre of her being wanted him, every cell of her brain, every throbbing pulse, every half-dreamed memory and unplanned flight of imagination combined to scream her desire for him . . . But she wanted him for ever, not just one night.

Forcefully, she gathered the two parts of her shirt together, pushed away from him, and sat up. 'No,' she managed tightly. And again, *'No!'*

She felt the bed shift with his weight, and without turning knew that he sat on the other side, his back to her. There was an endless, intense silence, broken only by the sounds of her own staccato breathing, filled with the pain of broken promises and what-might-have-been, the ache of desire which would never know its ultimate . . . Then Byron spoke to the wall opposite.

'What,' he said deeply, fiercely, 'do you want from a man, Dawn?'

Somehow she found her voice. 'Foreverness,' she managed, in only a half-whisper. 'Security, and . . . foreverness.'

He stood abruptly. 'Not much!'

He stalked to her side of the bed and bent to pick up the candle. Its light reflected a face that was cold and angry and utterly remote. It was the face of a man who feels cheated because he is unprepared to pay the price.

Dawn forced strength into her legs and followed him across the room, her fingers woodenly and clumsily buttoning the blouse which revealed her shame. And as the sturdy wooden door closed behind them she was aware of a new and awful sadness. When one night was all that was offered, perhaps it was better, in the end, than nothing at all.

CHAPTER SEVEN

THE relationship was back to an impersonal, business-as-usual one between Dawn and Byron. Once made and so humiliatingly rejected, to attempt to move it on to a different level would not be repeated. Dawn kept assuring herself she had done the right thing, but inside her sense of self-doubt was growing. To have submitted to him on those terms would have proved him right—that she was the type of girl capable of seeking and taking romance in the form of a quick, casual affair in a faraway land, expecting and offering nothing more. It was respect for her own self-image which would never allow her to believe that about herself. But in another way, she had already proven Byron right: She had led him on, her instincts had betrayed her—he must have known from the moment that door closed behind them how she felt. And once again, at the last moment, she had backed away, withholding promises. She could understand his fury and disgust with her, and was grateful to him for not allowing it to show. That was his own self-respect.

The castle was a flurry of activity for the festival to be held at the end of the week. Workmen began at the break of day, building tables and digging roasting pits in the courtyard. A score of girls from the village were hired to clean the castle from top to bottom, and every day from dawn to dusk each corner was filled with the delicious smells of baking bread and a myriad delightful sweets.

Dawn had a sudden stab of poignant longing for what the castle must be like at Christmas; the towering fir tree, the ancient yule log, the warm, spicy smells, all the villagers gathering to pass the wassail bowl and sing their traditional songs. She knew that when the seasons turned and Park Avenue was bright with tinsel and lights and screaming traffic, part of her would be here, beside the huge roaring fire, listening to the laughter and the chattering of strange tongues, and looking for Byron's face.

She tried to pitch in and help Maggie as much as she could, in return for her hospitality. The only remaining pictures she planned to take were of the festival, and of the construction site if the murky sky ever cleared enough to allow the kind of shot she had in mind, and so, except for the typing of her notes, her work was all but completed. And she did enjoy working with the other girls in the huge, stone-floored kitchen, putting her hands into dough and getting flour smeared on her face and feeling she really belonged.

'This couldn't have been more perfectly timed,' confided Maggie one afternoon as they worked side by side at the cutting board, chopping dried fruit. 'Hilary is leaving for the mainland the day after the festival, and Byron has to make a decision before then. I'm hoping that, on a night traditional for its good will and high spirits, he might be moved at the last minute to change his mind.'

Dawn enquired, 'Why does he have to make a decision before she leaves?'

'Thomas Mann has a contract that's re-negotiable every year—and it expires on Thursday night. I know it's rather unusual to have a partnership under those terms, but over the years it's become more of a tradition than anything else, the renewal. This year I don't think Byron is planning to renew.'

Dawn ventured, 'Vernon thinks it would be a mistake—from a business standpoint.'

'Oh, it would,' agreed Maggie. 'It would mean a tremendous financial loss, not to mention the physical burden it would place on Byron. He really can't handle everything by himself. It's too much for any one man.'

Dawn could not help but wonder at the type of man who would make such a sacrifice for the sake of principle.

'Oh, dear!' Maggie looked up suddenly. 'I almost forgot. The workmen needed Byron to show them where to put the torch stands before they can go any further. Would you mind finding him, dear, and telling him? I believe he might still be in his office with Vernon.'

'Sure thing.' Dawn wiped her hands on a towel and steeled herself for the first face-to-face encounter she had had with Byron since that rainy night in the tower room.

The door to his office was open, so she did not have to make the decision as to whether to interrupt and risk his wrath. As she peeped cautiously inside, she saw him leaning back in his chair with his feet on the desk, strumming the guitar lightly. Vernon was in a chair beside the desk, half facing the door, and busy with a pocket calculator, but he saw her first. 'Oh, Dawn.' He greeted her with a smile. 'You wanted to see Byron? Don't mind me; we've finished. Come on in.'

She stepped inside, and Byron placed the guitar beside the desk, swinging his feet down, leaning forward in the chair and looking at her. 'Maggie said——' She began, and almost forgot her message. Something about torches. 'Maggie said the workmen need you to tell them where to put the torch holders. They can't go any further until you do.'

'Oh, what a bore!' He leaned back in the chair and half-closed his eyes. 'Vernon, you go. You remember where they were last year, and besides, I'm expecting Hilary at any moment.'

Hilary. That was a shock. Dawn said, a little stiffly, 'Well, if you're expecting someone I won't keep you . . .'

'Was there something else?' He lifted an eyebrow curiously.

'No.' She turned. 'Nothing else.'

Vernon said, 'Nice seeing you again, Dawn,' as he passed, and she started to make her own escape just as she heard Byron's voice again.

'Hilary is coming over to pick up some papers . . . the up-to-date accounts, the final figures her father will need to wind up his part of the partnership.'

She did not know why he should bother explaining to her, but she half-turned, and managed vaguely, 'Oh.' Then, 'So you've definitely made up your mind.'

He eyed her frankly. 'You don't approve, do you?'

On the verge of answering, she retreated. 'It's really none of my business,' she began.

'There are a great many things in this castle which are none of your business,' he returned caustically, 'but you manage to have an opinion on them nonetheless. So let me hear it.'

Stung, she replied, 'As a matter of fact, I do think you're acting rather childish.'

He lifted a cool eyebrow. 'Childish, is it?'

'Yes,' she continued imperviously, 'childish. I've never believed in allowing—emotions to get in the way of business, and I think you're too smart to let something like this cloud your judgment. In the first place, your personal life should be entirely separate from your business life. And in the second, I think what you're really doing is trying to punish Hilary for what she did to you. Of course the only two people you're really hurting are the innocent parties—yourself, and Thomas Mann. That,' she finished, proud of her courage, 'is childish.'

He drawled, 'I ask for an opinion, and I get a lecture. Thank you, Miss Morrison.' And suddenly his eyes strayed over her shoulder. 'Good afternoon.'

Dawn turned to meet Hilary, stunning in a green wool sheath dress with an amber chiffon scarf fastened at her throat with a topaz pin. The colours flattered her smooth red hair and her green catlike eyes, and she moved past Dawn with a light laugh and a look which made her feel as though she was one of the village girls hired to do the house. 'What have they done, my dear,' she said, her eyes raking her up and down in amusement, 'hired you out as kitchen help?'

Dawn was aware of the apron she had forgotten to remove over her flour-dusted jeans, and she blushed. Then Byron explained, an undertone of amusement in his voice, 'You have a streak of flour across your nose,' and the flush became scarlet.

She said, with what she hoped was a modicum of dignity, 'If you'll excuse me, I think I'll go— wash my face,' and fled the room wretchedly,

She wondered if Hilary had been standing there

long enough to hear Dawn's own hot defence of her. That would make her humiliation complete.

She went back miserably to help Maggie in the kitchen, and they watched the work in the courtyard from the large window, open against the heat from the ovens. It was another grey, misty day, the mountains and even the tops of trees in the distance were obscured by clouds, and Dawn wondered, 'What happens if it rains?'

'Oh,' Maggie replied cheerfully, 'that won't dampen anyone's spirits one bit. We'll have canopies rigged to be raised at a moment's notice, and of course there's plenty of room in the castle for those who are afraid they'll melt! Actually, we usually do have a shower or two every festival; it doesn't spoil a thing. They say it's very romantic, under the canopies, with the rain beating down.' Her glance carried a suggestion of a message, but it was quickly gone as she turned to place a tray of pastries in the oven.

'You know,' she continued, scooping out a large lump of dough on to the flour-covered board and beginning to knead it vigorously, 'that the festival had its origins in a pagan love ritual.'

Dawn shook her head and regarded her with interest.

'Oh, sure. It's part of the vernal equinox—of course, you'll notice it's held later now, purely for climactical reasons, I suspect!—and the vernal equinox, or first day of spring, is traditionally associated with fertility, both of the land and the human race. I don't want to scare you off by suggesting orgies on the lawn, or anything of the sort, but romance is definitely in the air. They say the birth rate goes up twenty per cent nine months to the day after the Spring Festival ...' She chuckled. 'I don't know. I do know that a girl is more likely to be proposed to that night than any other of the year—and many's the happy life that began under a canopy on the lawn of Falkone's Acres. Which reminds me.' She looked up, 'we'll have to see what we can do about getting you a costume.'

'Costume?' parroted Dawn, her mind already racing ahead with some dread to a night filled with romance and she, alone, on the outside looking in.

'Oh, yes, indeed. We all dress in costumes. Heaven knows how it got started, because no one remembers ever seeing anything like them ever worn on the island ... I suspect Druid origins, although that's pretty far-fetched. They're a lot like togas, for men and women, but so colourful and romantic ... well, you'll just have to wait and see. We'll find something really spectacular for you. With your figure and long hair you'll look like something that stepped right out of the pages of a fairy book.'

Through the kitchen window, Dawn watched Hilary cross the yard towards the garage, a manilla portfolio under her arm. Well, thought Dawn in some surprise, that didn't take long! She looked vainly for some sign of Byron, and started guiltily at the sound of his voice behind her.

'Don't bother about Dawn's costume, Mags,' he said, and then turned to her. 'If you think you can tear yourself away from here for a minute,' he said crisply, 'I'd like to talk to you.'

With an awful tightening in her chest and a sinking in the pit of her stomach, Dawn washed her hands and dried them, remembering to take off the apron and to check her face for smudges in the reflection of the window. He was going to ask her to leave, now, today. She had finally gone too far, and he was going to ask her to leave.

She followed him dully out of the kitchen and into the empty corridor. He said abruptly, 'You've about finished with your work, haven't you?'

It was terrible, this physical hold he had on her. The way merely being in his presence could set her stomach to churning and her hands to trembling; his dark eyes, even when they were cold, as they were now, compelling her to come closer, making her want to touch. Would she never forget the way his arms felt around her, his warm breath on her neck, the powerful swell and tightening of his muscles . . . would she always long for it to be that way again?

She answered, nervously, 'Yes . . . almost. There's still the festival, which I think is very important . . . I would really like to stay for the festival.' But she would not beg.

He looked surprised. 'And why shouldn't you? You're not scheduled to leave until Sunday, are you?'

'No,' she answered, confused. 'But just now, when you told Maggie not to bother . . . I thought you might want me to leave sooner.'

Byron looked impatient. 'I meant *I* would see to your costume. Maggie has enough to do.'

'Then,' she queried hesitantly, overwhelmed with relief, 'what did you want to talk to me about?'

'I want to see what you've done so far,' he announced, with more of an air of a command than a request.

'You mean my photographs?' She spread her hands helplessly. 'I'm afraid that's impossible. I would be glad to send you the proofs before they go to press, if that would help, but that's the best I can do.'

He shook his head in annoyance. 'I want to see them before you leave.'

'But they're undeveloped!'

'Can't you develop film?' he demanded.

'Well, of course I could, if I had the equipment!'

'Then,' he commanded imperiously, 'get your film and come with me.'

She had to go all the way up to her room to collect the film, still puzzling over what Byron had in mind and his autocratic reasons for it. When she rejoined him in the hall he led the way back through the kitchen, across an exposed wooden porch, and into a small room lit by a red light, equipped with two huge sinks, a counter, a drying rack, and smelling wonderfully of familiar chemicals.

'A darkroom!' she exclaimed.

'An old washroom,' he corrected. 'But I think it will suit. I checked with the chemist on the mainland to make sure you had everything you needed. If I overlooked anything, just let me know.'

She turned to him. In the weird light his face looked detached, impersonal, like a memory floating through a dream. She said, 'I had no idea there was a darkroom in the castle. Why didn't you tell me?'

'Because it was only completed this morning,' he replied.

'What a terrible expense for only one use!' she blurted, forgetting that expense would mean nothing to him.

She cursed the unrevealing light for masking his expression as he tipped his head towards her. 'Oh,

I think it will be worth it,' he answered. 'I may have the opportunity to use it again.' He opened the door. 'I want to see them as soon as you're done.'

Dawn spent the afternoon in the fantasy world of chemicals and colours, watching the cold film come to life under the magic of her fingers. Chronicled before her she saw a wistful account of her life from the very first moment she had arrived here—it seemed like another world ago. The pink patch of thrift growing in the woods, heralding the gateway to adventure, the colours so true and vibrant she could almost touch them. The frontal view of the castle, rising majestically on the knoll, the ferocious carved lions, every detail sharp and clear in the sunlight. She had done a double exposure of the Boyd crest overlaid on a telescopic view of the castle, and the effect was magnificent. There was a shot looking dizzily down the tower staircase, with high-intensity lighting showing dust motes dancing in the air and sharp contrasts of shadows and light meant to give the impression, as it did, that one was being watched. Atmosphere. The commercial shots of the guest rooms and facilities she skipped over, thinking with true regret that those were probably the ones the magazine would give the most attention to. The garden colours were brilliant and true, taken at midday with the mountains in the background so close one could almost touch them. Then there were the pictures of the island . . . the dark forests, the misty, snow-capped mountains, the grey beach and churning surf, the rugged cliffs. The still blue lochs, the placid meadows, and the ones she liked the best, the colourful street scenes from the village. Here she had let her penchant for character shots run wild, and captured what she thought was the essence of the little town. The vendor with his wagon, the musician with his mandolin, the girls huddled together before a fuchsia-pink shop front, giggling and whispering. A tall, rugged farmer boy plodding along on a horse. Housewives with stern, stoic features haggling at the fish market, and young men in tweeds pedalling by on bicycles. The collections of bottles on the office wall of the distillery, reflecting centuries of island prosperity, the dark, truer-than-life shots of the inner workings of the distillery itself, evoking strong odours and unpleasant sensations, but nevertheless a part of the whole. The magazine, she reflected again regretfully, would never use those. They were too intense. And finally was her cover shot, the castle brilliant in the sunlight, reflected in detail in the black pool at its base, surrounded by brilliant greenery and colourful borders. On the whole, she was very pleased, and could take them to Byron with self-confidence and a slight touch of professional pride.

They met in his office, and he spread them out over the desk, scrutinising each one in silence. Even though she knew they were good and her own opinion, as her editor was constantly telling her, was the only one that mattered, she found her annoyance growing with nervousness through his lengthy, scowling, intense examination. Why, she began to defend herself irritably, should he demand to see her work before even her editor did? She was not working for him! Did he have some insane notion that his power extended to censoring her work before she left the island? How dared he! What did he know about photography, anyway? What conception could he have of the hours of work which went into lighting and posing and arranging and re-shooting before she got that one perfect shot? What did he know of the years of training which went into being able to capture on film an idea, a concept, a way of thinking? He had no right to disapprove so arrogantly of anything she had done.

When at last Byron glanced up at her she tensed in her chair, ready to spring like a tiger defending its young. Then he said, looking down at the spread again, 'Dawn, this is magnificent!'

The breath went out of her in one sudden, inaudible gasp.

He continued in a subdued, almost awed, tone, 'I mean it. You've captured things here I would have thought even a native might have missed. It's—the character of the island. Not just places, things . . . but it lives and breathes right here before me. I don't know what else to say.' He looked at her, his eyes glowing softly. 'This is it . . . the place I love, the place I know as well as I know my own body . . . you've discovered it. I could almost say you must love it as much as I do.'

She answered shyly, 'I think I do. At least I've tried to show what I feel with the camera.'

He smiled, and that one shared moment sent a tingle of warmth through Dawn which was worth it all. If she never took another photograph again, that one moment was worth it all, for it seemed she had waited her entire life to hear those exact words of praise, to see in that one dark pair of eyes approval, and pride.

Then he asked, 'Do you mind if I keep these for a while?'

'Oh, no,' she replied generously. 'They're yours to keep, if you like. I've got the negatives.'

He nodded, glancing at them again. 'Good. Will you do the text to go along with them yourself?'

She nodded. 'Not much. Just an intro and a few lines per picture. The idea for a magazine such as ours is to let the pictures speak for themselves.'

'And they certainly do that,' he agreed. 'Yes, they certainly do.' He favoured her with a teasing half-smile. 'Now, you see, I'm not such an ogre. I'm pretty harsh with my criticism, but I can give honest praise when it's deserved. Maybe it's just that I'm a perfectionist.'

'Well, then, I suppose I should be flattered.' And she was. Deeply.

Byron told her seriously, 'I never flatter.' Then, with an abrupt change of subject, 'It's too bad you'll be working the night of the festival. I don't think you can really get involved in it from behind the lens of a camera.' He glanced at her, and the expression on his lips twisted to mocking challenge. 'But I forget. You don't *want* to get involved, do you?'

She replied, coolly, the moment spoiled, 'I have a job to do.'

'Someone could do you a big favour,' he answered with sudden low ferocity, 'by slipping you a couple of stiff whiskies and making you forget, even if just for one night, that damn job.'

Dawn replied with an airiness she did not feel, rising, 'I hope that person would be prepared to support me for the rest of my life, then, because I need that "damn job" to keep the wolf away from my door!'

Byron leaned back in his chair, templing his fingers, unpleasant mirth dancing in his eyes. 'Why, Miss Morrison,' he drawled, 'is that a proposal?'

She flushed scarlet, and could not think of a suitably flippant reply. She merely answered, 'No,' and went in one moment from a sophisticated, successful career woman to an awkward, stammering schoolgirl whose only desire was to escape that room and the mocking eyes of the man she was afraid to love.

He drawled, 'How disappointing!' and began gathering up the photographs. Without looking at her again, he added, 'I've got some work to do now, so if you'll excuse me . . .'

Dawn felt like a toy puppet who had been made to dance for the amusement of royalty, whose strings had been cut and tossed away as her antics ceased to amuse.

The remaining days before the festival were filled with busy activity, and Dawn threw herself into it automatically. Anything to avoid facing the fact that in only a matter of days she must leave, draw the curtain over a segment of her life which would never be completely ended, and try, somehow, never to look back. Life was cruel, and she had not lived twenty-five years without discovering that, but she simply had never felt it more acutely than on that bright, clear morning of the festival. Only a few more hours and it would all be over. Saturday would be spent packing and saying her polite goodbyes, and Sunday would see her on a plane over the Atlantic, leaving behind more of herself than she could afford to lose.

Byron met her at the entrance to the dining room, an envelope in his hand. 'This has just come for you,' he said. 'It looks important.'

There was the horror everyone feels when first presented with a telegram, combined with a sinking fear as she scanned the heading. 'It's—

from my editor,' she managed shakily. What had happened? Had Byron called her bluff and telephoned her editor to complain? Was this a stiff dismissal and a demand that she return immediately? Why else would he telegraph her . . .

She scanned it quickly, and then again, to make certain she had read correctly: 'Dawn Stop. Loved the photos. Stop. Try a Sketch on the Hebrides. Stop. Take Two Weeks. Stop. Joe.'

She let the paper go limp in her hands and stared at Byron as though he somehow could hold the answer to the puzzle. 'He—wants me to stay in the island. Do a thing on the Hebrides.' She asked incredulously, '*What* photos?'

Byron replied casually, 'I hope you don't mind, but I sent them over by express post with a— rather complimentary note. I thought your editor might see the wisdom in doing a complete spread on the Hebrides, as long as you were here and seemed to have such an—affinity with the islands.'

'Do you mean,' she ventured, hardly daring to believe it, 'that this was your idea?'

Byron lifted his shoulders negligently. 'I might have suggested something. I don't really recall.'

'Oh!' She turned quickly so that he could not see the sudden joy which had leapt into her face. Two weeks! Two more weeks in the gorgeous Scottish Isles, and critical acclaim from her editor. Two more weeks that much nearer to Byron. Within commuting distance, with Falkone's Acres as her base point. Not leaving at all, no goodbyes . . . it was all too much for her to accept at once.

But above it all was the soaring knowledge that it had been Byron's idea. He *wanted* her to stay. He wanted it so badly that he had gone to all this trouble with her editor to arrange it. She *was* welcome here!

There was no purer joy than to know, for the first time in her life, that she belonged. And no sweeter pain than to hope, somehow, some day, to belong to this man. And to believe, for the first time, that he might hope the same thing.

CHAPTER EIGHT

ALL day long people were in and out, bringing dishes of cooked and uncooked food, table settings and cutlery. It was more like a well-organised family reunion than the impromptu pagan festival it was advertised to be, but, explained Maggie, 'We would have absolute chaos if we didn't have someone calling the shots. Things will get disorganised enough tonight after the sun goes down and the whisky starts flowing!'

It was not until luncheon, served late because of the schedule, that Dawn had a chance to propose, very casually, her idea. 'Since I'm going to be here in the islands another few weeks,' she said, 'and Falkone's Acres is rather centrally located, it would really be convenient for me if I could use the castle as sort of a base of operations, and continue to stay here when I'm not exploring.' She glanced at Maggie anxiously. 'If you don't mind, that is.'

Byron looked up with a mischievous twinkle. 'Our first paying guest. How about that, Mags?'

Maggie shot him a quelling glance. 'Paying guest, indeed!' She turned to Dawn. 'Of course you'll stay here, my dear, as our *personal* guest. I wouldn't have it any other way.'

'You'll never make a profit that way,' observed Byron perversely, and turned back to his meal.

'The magazine,' Dawn told him, 'will pay you out of my per-diem.'

'You'll need to arrange some method of getting

back and forth between the islands,' he reminded her. 'The ferry's base point is in Oban.'

'She'll use one of our boats,' Maggie supplied. 'You can spare a man to take her around.'

'No, really,' protested Dawn. 'That's too inconvenient . . .'

'I'll think about it,' replied Byron, 'and let you know how inconvenient it is.'

She did not resent him for attempting to make things as difficult as possible for her. In all fairness, she had not made things particularly easy for him in the past, and he deserved a chance to get even. But she had two more weeks to correct the injustices of the past, which was more than she had had yesterday. And no matter what he did or said to make her doubt his motives, nothing could change the fact that those two weeks were made possible only because of him.

In the afternoon young men and women began to bring in wagonloads of wild flowers and boughs of greenery which Maggie showed her how to wind into garlands which would be tacked up around the courtyard on trees and canopy poles. So far the day was clear if a little hazy, warm but certainly not hot. The fragrance of the fresh cut flowers and sap-laden branches wafted over the courtyard deliciously as she sat cross-legged on the grass in the midst of the other laughing, flirtatious couples, working with florist's wire and tape to construct natural-looking arrangements out of the materials piled around her. She made a friend out of a twelve year-old boy, the tag-along little brother of one of the girls, and he sat faithfully at her feet, patiently weaving a garland of wild flowers for her crown. She graciously accepted his shy offering and allowed him to place it on her head, and they worked happily together the rest of the afternoon.

Late in the afternoon Byron stopped by, and he scowled as he noticed her sitting there, laughing and talking with the other couples. 'Where did you get that?' he demanded, gesturing to the garland.

'Oh,' she replied casually, feeling he deserved to be teased, 'an admirer.'

'It was me, sir,' piped up little Sean, spoiling the joke, and Dawn was not sorry. She did not want his temper to spoil the evening.

His black expression lightened. 'Best be careful,' he remarked to her before moving on. 'People have become engaged for less than that.'

Noticing the time, she left not long after that. Washing her hair was a major project, and even with the assistance of her electric blow-drier, it would take hours to dry.

Byron met her on the way to the shower, as she had done to him once before. The only difference was that she was swathed in a floor-length terry houserobe and she should have felt no reason for embarrassment. It was the way he looked at her hair, loose down her back, that brought back his husky, adoring words, 'Bedroom hair . . .' And she thought he, too, was remembering the way it had looked against the pillow of his grandparents' old-fashioned canopy bed.

She started to move past him, for the look was too uncomfortable to maintain for long, but he said abruptly, 'Why did you never cut it?'

She turned back to him. 'I—beg your pardon?'

'Your hair,' he answered curtly. 'You're so careful to disguise everything about you that's feminine, why the vanity with your hair?'

It was a question that had no answer, and she simply stared at him, flustered.

'I'll tell you why you do it,' he answered his own question in a low tone, his eyes not on her face but on the pattern her hair traced from the slight opening of the robe between the mound of her breasts, the belt at the slim waist, the outline of her thighs, the curve of her hips. 'It's because you know it drives men mad, and being a woman, you can't stop exercising whatever perverse power you have over them.'

'That—is ridiculous,' she defended, stammering. 'It has nothing to do with——'

Almost, a smile graced his full, sensuous lips. 'Ah, yes, Dawn love,' he murmured caressingly. 'You're more of a woman than you think. And one day you're going to allow me to show you just how much of a woman that is.'

He turned and went into his room, and she was left alone in the corridor, her chest tight with the implication of his promise, flushing with anticipation and shivering with dread. She would never understand what motivated his male mind, nor follow his drastic swings of mood. He had been angry enough to kill that night they had left the bedchamber, passions unconsummated, promises unfulfilled. Yet he had sent lavish praise to her editor and arranged for her to stay in the islands, then immediately acted as though it were immaterial to him whether she stayed or not. One moment he was cool and impersonal, the next intimidating her with his disturbingly suggestive sexuality and thinly disguised passion. It was a delightful whirlwind with which he had captured her mind, but one thing still bothered her, kept her from running into his arms as her instincts urged her to do, forced her to keep her composure and her emotions under control. Byron knew her terms, and he had not yet made a move to suggest conceding to them. The attraction he felt for her was still entirely physical. And perhaps it would always be.

When she returned to her room there was a garment laid out on her bed, and she gasped in delight as she went over to it. Maggie had been right in describing the costumes as romantic, but she had not suggested they were also revealing, suggestive, and utterly sensual. Considering the theme of the festival, Dawn supposed, as she lifted it delicately and pressed it to her, it was only fitting.

It was fashioned in a medieval style out of layers of azure gauze with a wide silver cincture at the waist. It was scooped low over the shoulders and flowed to floor-length caftan sleeves, each layer of the shimmering gauze so thin it was practically translucent in itself, placed together it formed the illusion of billowing fullness over unmistakable nudity. Dawn was glad it would be dark.

Then she noticed that the colours—silver and azure—were those of the Boyd standard. She wondered if that were significant.

By the time she dried her hair and applied a minimum of make-up it was already dark, and she could hear in the distance the musical chanting of hundreds of voices. Intrigued, she went to the window in her robe and watched the small trail of winding torches grow closer and more brilliant, along with the feral rhythm of the chant—basses like the pounding of drums, sopranos and tenors blending into wild counterpoint, and its chords touched something untamed and basic in her, set her blood to racing hotly, sent a shiver down her spine. She turned quickly from the window to finish dressing.

It was apparent that the costume was not meant to be worn over a bra, slip, or chemisette, and she wondered in alarm if anything *at all* was supposed to be worn under it. When she slipped it on she blushed at her own reflection. Nothing whatsoever was left to the imagination. It was cut so low that it barely covered the rosy tips of her nipples, so wide that white shoulders and most of her back were exposed, and so tight across the bodice that her firm, rounded breasts were pressed together beneath a shockingly deep cleavage, and thrust forward in such a provocative manner that it put her immediately in mind of old movies reflecting the lascivious lives of medieval lords and ladies. She wondered perversely if Byron had not deliberately left out some essential part of the costume, and rummaged through her closet for a shawl.

Because the costume, even with its demure white shawl, seemed to require it, she left her hair loose, braiding a few strands on either side of her face and allowing the remainder to cascade down her back. She whirled around once in the room, loving the way the gauze billowed and floated about her body, and then there was a knock on the door.

She tugged once more at the unco-operative neckline, drew the shawl more closely about her, and went to answer it.

Byron was there, looking so much like the handsome prince every girl dreams about that Dawn drew her breath in surprise and appreciation. His costume was a loose-fitting garment of a white homespun material which fell just below the thighs, open to the waist where it was the perfect

frame for the broad chest with its alluringly
masculine cushion of dark, curly hair. A width of
soft azure wool was thrown over one shoulder and
fastened at the waist with a silver cincture similar
to the one she wore. His arms were bare, offering
her the first glimpse she had ever had of firmly-
muscled biceps. His knees and thighs were swathed
in dark stockings, accenting their sturdy shape and
alluring masculinity much more effectively than if
they had been bare, and he wore leather boots
laced to the knee.

He swept her a courtly bow. 'My lady,' he
drawled.

Dawn responded, somewhat timorously, because
her heart was pounding in her throat, 'My lord,'
and knelt in a curtsey.

He bent to lift her to her feet and as he did he
swept the shawl from her shoulders. The movement
revealed the dark tuft of hair under each arm
which was both intimate and somehow exciting,
and her blush deepened as he gazed at her with
frank approval. 'This is no time for modesty, my
dear,' he said, and opening her door, he tossed the
shawl inside. 'You wouldn't want to draw
attention to yourself by being overdressed.'

'I hardly think there's any chance of that,' she
murmured, and because she could no longer
endure his unabashed examination of her bosom,
she turned towards the lift. 'Which reminds me,'
she continued to direct the conversation away
from a possible dangerous turn, 'of something I've
always meant to ask you. Are you really a lord? I
mean, should I call you that? What is your title?'

'Mister,' he replied, though there was amusement
in his eyes as he pushed the lift button which
suggested he read her motives for changing the

subject, and would humour her—for a time. 'The title died out centuries ago, for all the difference it makes.'

They stepped into the lift, and once again she was overwhelmingly aware of his masculinity and nearness. Perhaps now it was more powerful than ever because the trappings of civilisation—the carefully styled hair, the tailored suits, the scent of cologne—were gone, leaving only the basic, rugged man, all the more exciting for its simplicity. 'Are you aware,' he began conversationally, as the lift made its silent descent, 'that in medieval times, right up through the eighteenth century, the bosom was the focal point of a man's attraction to a woman? Frontal nudity was quite the fashion then, and some of the literature of the era in praise of that particular portion of a woman's anatomy is quite shocking by today's standards. We tend to think of our ancestors as stodgy and puritanical, as though they were all born under Queen Victoria, when in fact quite the opposite is true. In my father's day the costumes were much more authentic—and daring. It was the high point of every little boy's life when he got to attend his first festival.'

She commented, trying not to tug too obviously at the neckline, 'I can't imagine anything more daring.'

But Byron noticed the gesture and caught her hand, his fingers like a brush of flame for just the briefest instant across her bare skin. 'If I showed you the photographs of one of my father's festivals,' he assured her, his eyes laughing, 'you'd think they're pornographic.'

They emerged into the foyer, where the open door already revealed a party in full swing, the torches in the trees bathing the lawn in a vibrant orange light, dancing off the garlands of wild flowers, the flowing garments of dancers whirling madly in a circle, flickering on the long tables already piled high with food. The music was loud and untamed, occasionally punctuated by high laughter or a girlish squeal, and as they stepped out on to the portico Dawn could see the flame dancing in Byron's eyes, could feel the excitement course through him which was the essence of this place, this time. Although already she could sense his attention straying from her, his last words of advice were, 'Let go. Give it a chance. Enjoy yourself,' before he left her, taking the steps in majestic bounds, like a little boy let out of school for the day.

There was a group of women gathered on the steps, and she made her way absently towards them, feeling left out and rather slighted. How, she wondered morosely, could she enjoy herself if he was not there? For the first time she realised she had forgotten her camera, and she turned to go back upstairs for it.

Then her eyes fell on Byron—standing in the centre of the lawn, arms outstretched for a buxom young girl with flowers in her hair who was running towards him. He caught her up, whirled her around, and kissed her. Setting her feet on the ground, he caught another girl, tilted her backwards with one arm, and kissed her. He had not even released her before he caught the hand of another. Dawn watched, stunned, then heard Maggie's laughter and felt her arm slip through hers.

'It's traditional,' she explained. 'The lord of the castle is expected to kiss every unmarried girl present before the stroke of midnight, at risk of losing his virility and his harvest the next year.'

'Of course,' drawled a low feminine voice in her other ear, 'the rule used to be that he must kiss only virgins, but they've become so hard to find, you know.'

Dawn turned to face Hilary, her red lips upturned in her usual mocking smile, her glittering eyes narrowed seductively. She seemed to have an uncanny knack for matching her outfits to her environment, as though purposely requiring her clothing to take a back seat to her own striking beauty. The amber gown she wore blended into the flickering torchlight so that she seemed herself an extension of the flame, her gold collar its core, her red hair its tip. The filmy material did not billow gracefully about her as did Dawn's, but fell in a single clinging layer from the scooped neckline to her bare ankles. It was deliberately provocative in its construction, suiting a woman such as Hilary to perfection, and, although she may have worn a low underskirt, it was patently translucent from bosom to navel, and Dawn found herself looking away in embarrassment. Only Hilary could get away with that!

Hilary touched her arm lightly. 'One piece of advice, if I may, Miss—I do beg your pardon, dear, I can't seem to recall your name.'

'Morrison,' returned Dawn shortly. 'Dawn Morrison.'

'Yes, of course. As I was saying . . .' Hilary nodded towards the scene before them, in which Byron was the centre of attention from every silly, squealing girl present, 'Byron reserves the right of jealousy exclusively to himself. Don't let on to him that this sort of thing bothers you. He despises a mistrustful woman.'

She moved gracefully down the steps, and Dawn

stared after her in shock and indignation. Of all people to be giving *her* advice on how to handle Byron—speaking so impudently of loyalty and mistrust! As though ... as though she was graciously abdicating her territory to a lesser woman!

Maggie patted her arm reassuringly. 'Don't mind Hilary,' she said. 'There's not a woman here who wouldn't like to claw her eyes out.' Maggie's tone indicated that she might like to be one of them. Then, urging her down the steps. 'Come along, have some fun.' There was a suggestive twinkle in her eyes. 'Don't forget—*you're* an unmarried woman!'

Dawn thought belligerently, descending the steps proudly, As though I would want—or accept—his kiss on those cheap terms!

'I've been saving this for you.' She turned in surprise and then some pleasure to meet Vernon, who was shyly offering her a garland of flowers. 'Your costume is incomplete without it.'

She allowed him to place it on her head, then stepped back for his approval.

'Beautiful,' he said, his eyes glowing like those of a worshipful schoolboy. 'I mean it, Dawn. You look—incredible tonight. Like one of those paintings you see of castle life.'

She laughed, revelling in his appreciation. Never mind that it was not *his* praise she sought.

He gestured around him to include the lights, the costumes, the music, the dancing and the laughter. 'What do you think?'

'It's all so—wild, and primitive,' she replied, then smiled. 'I think I like it.'

'Will you dance with me?'

She eyed the other dancers executing the

intricate, weaving patterns of a folk dance, and demurred, 'I don't know the steps.'

'All you have to do is follow me. It's more instinct than anything.' He had taken her hand. 'I'll show you.'

Her eyes had fallen at that moment on Byron, and it was Hilary standing before him, Hilary's arms gently encircling his neck. His back was to her, so that Dawn could not see the expression on his face, but she did see him bend his neck, his hands on her shoulders, and kiss her. And it seemed to her his lips lingered longer than they had with any of the other girls.

She said brightly, turning back to Vernon, 'Sure—all right. I'll give it a try.'

Happily, he tucked her arm through his and led her towards a group which was just assembling into formation for another set. 'There's nothing to it, really. It's not something you can learn, you just have to follow the music . . .'

He was interrupted by a mild voice behind him, and a hand light upon his shoulder.

'This is my dance, I believe,' said Byron.

Vernon looked uncertainly from him to Dawn, and then agreed, dropping his arm, 'Yes, I believe it is. Sorry, I didn't notice.'

Dawn said angrily, as he left them, 'What do you mean—your dance? You didn't ask me!'

He replied blandly, 'You're wearing my colours. It means you're not allowed to dance with any other man but me.'

'Which means,' she retorted bitterly, 'that I don't get to dance at all!'

'That's up to you,' he replied, unruffled. 'I can always find someone else.'

She stared at him. 'Why is there one rule for you

and another for me?'

'Because,' he answered, securely anchoring her arm in his, 'you're a woman. Now, do you want to dance or not?'

'It seems to me,' she muttered discontentedly, 'that you have this whole thing rigged to suit you very well!'

He laughed. 'The French have a phrase for it— *droit du seigneur*. It means——'

'I know what it means,' she retorted. 'It means that the lord of the castle must have everything he wants——'

'And every woman,' he added, and they had reached the formation as the first notes were being struck. 'Shall I ask you one more time or merely take you whether you like it or not? It is my right.'

For a moment she was shocked, not under-standing his meaning, and his eyes caught her confusion and danced madly. Then she cried angrily above the rising chords of the music, 'Yes, I want to dance!'

Byron whirled her into step, his strong hands gripping hers and swinging her around in rhythm to the music, swaying in motion with the other couples, and it was easy. The music was loud and compulsive, his touch masterful, and her skirts billowed above her knees as she whirled and ducked and abandoned herself completely to the music. As it ended in squeals of laughter and shouts of applause, he caught her at the waist and whirled her around, feet above ground, then pressed his lips fiercely to hers. 'There!' he declared, setting her down. 'I've kissed the last single girl and possibly the only virgin present, and my land and my potential for progeny are secure for another year!'

Dawn had time to reflect that, in the eerie light, with his crisp dark hair and lips parted in laughter over gleaming white teeth, he looked incredibly like a satyr. And then he left her.

They sat on low cushions around the table to eat, the women on one side, the men on another, each group separated by about ten yards of lawn and two heavily laden buffet tables. 'Now this,' Dawn pointed out laughingly to Maggie, 'is not very romantic.'

'Oh, but it's the best part!' Maggie insisted. 'They're looking us over,' she confided, nodding at the men who did not appear to be looking at anything but their plates. 'Choosing their partners. When we've finished eating, all the women will go out to prepare the draught—that's sort of a whisky punch—and while we're gone different colours straws will be passed out among the men. Finding a broken straw under her napkin when she returns means that a girl has a secret lover— and all she has to do then is find the owner of the other half of the straw! It's such fun the rest of the evening as the girls run around trying to find their lovers. Long ago,' she finished, 'the breaking of straws was part of the marriage ceremony. Some pople still take it that seriously . . . for others, it's all in good fun, or a chance for a shy lad to win his lass . . . however you look at it, it makes for anything other than a dull evening!'

Dawn concentrated on the rich, spicy food piled high on her plate and did not concern herself much with straws. Except to wonder if Hilary might find one under her napkin, and take it as a token of reconciliation. She could not forget the way he had kissed her, so different from her own kiss, brief and triumphant. It must be hard for a man to taste again the lips he had once loved, especially when they belonged to a woman as beautiful and seductive as Hilary. And she did not believe that Byron could have kissed her at all, not even for the sake of ceremony, if there were not something still there . . .

When the women rose to go to the castle kitchen Dawn followed them, although when she learned that they were expected to serve the men, cup by cup, she objected in principle, and she told Maggie so. She laughed it off. 'It's all part of the spirit, dearie. And,' she added with a wink. 'it's only for one night.'

The draught was a mixture of strong Scotch whisky, milk, beaten eggs and peppery spices, and then women were not allowed to taste. To this Dawn had no objection. They carried it out in huge tubs to the lawn, where it was dipped and served by each girl in a wooden cup. Dawn reflected that if all the mixture were consumed there would be a collection of either very drunk or very ill men before morning, and once again Maggie laughed it off. 'If a man can't hold his whisky he's not a man in these parts, and wouldn't last very long on the island.' She placed a cup in her hand and nodded towards the tables where the men were gathered. 'You must serve Byron,' she told her. 'Because you're wearing his colours, it would be an insult for any other girl to try to do it.'

She thought, damn these colours. Then she remembered that Byron had chosen them, possibly with this very humiliation in mind. 'What if I don't?' she demanded mutinously.

Maggie laughed. 'Better worry what would happen if he refuses. You would be in disgrace!'

So, thought Dawn, and approached his table with some trepidation. Maybe that was it. To get even with her for the fuss over the dance, or a thousand other things . . .

He was lying back on the grass, one arm cradling his head, a leg propped up to reveal an intriguing line of stocking-covered thigh above the boot.

The other girls were getting down on their knees, lifting their cups to the lips of their chosen ones. Dawn stood rigidly above him, the cup held tightly in both hands. 'I think this is a stupid and demeaning custom,' she said tightly.

His sparkling black eyes looked up at her lazily, amusement twitched at the corners of his lips. 'Do you mean to say,' he drawled comfortably, 'that you don't intend to get down on your knees before me?'

'That,' she replied with dignity, 'is exactly what I mean to say.'

'In the old days I could have you flogged for this,' he assured her.

Dawn was aware that others were watching. She felt colour warm her cheeks and she considered for the first time the embarrassment she might be causing Byron. He had honoured her by bestowing his colours upon her—hadn't he? And she was returning the honour by insulting a time-revered custom that really, after all, wasn't so important. She wished she hadn't been so stubborn about such a small matter—never mind that a principle was at stake—but she had gone too far to back down now. And it *was* the principle that was important. She had to defend it.

She said, 'These aren't the old days. Today men no longer see women as objects of servitude and don't try to make slaves of them. Today women are treated as equal partners in a relationship, and this entire little charade mocks that principle. A woman doesn't have to *serve* a man to show her respect for him, and I refuse to be a part of any custom that says differently.'

She was drawing a great deal of attention, she knew, but Byron seemed to be oblivious to it. By all accounts he should have been furious with her, both for insulting the custom and embarrassing him, but he did not appear to be either furious or embarrassed. He simply lifted an eyebrow mildly and murmured, 'It sounds as though I should be grateful you haven't thrown the cup in my face.'

Dawn was miserable with embarrassment and she wondered what would happen if she just turned and walked away. She would never be forgiven by the people of the island for insulting their custom—that much she knew, and why that should suddenly seem so important to her she did not know. Worse, she had insulted Byron and his standing in the community and she was really behaving very childishly. Was there any way she could apologise now without backing away from her stand?

But as he looked at her the mild amusement in his eyes gradually faded into something more serious, and he asked quietly, 'Do you have respect for me, Dawn?'

Respect. What an odd choice of words! Yet within his eyes was a meaning that was much deeper, a meaning so clear it took her breath away and she did not dare to believe it. It was a moment before she could manage, almost in a whisper, 'Yes.' Respect, and much more . . .

Byron got slowly to his feet, and his expression

in the flickering firelight was enigmatic. 'Then suppose,' he suggested softly, 'I meet you halfway?'

His hand closed about the cup, his eyes fastened upon hers, gently and without accusation ... perhaps even with admiration. Then he smiled, and his smile seemed to blossom within her and burst in her heart until she could not help returning it. Just before he drank he lifted the cup in a small, private salute to her, and through the glow of pleasure that thrilled her Dawn heard the surprised and approving murmurs go around the crowd. She returned to her table feeling as though she was walking on air.

There was a scurry of activity as the girls hastily began to search their napkins. Then there were moans of disappointment and squeals of delight, and to Dawn the entire atmosphere was like an Easter Egg hunt or Christmas morning.

She was still too lightheaded from the interlude with Byron to pay much attention to what was going on around her. She kept trying to catch a glimpse of him through the crowd, and then quickly looking away lest he catch her watching him. She hardly knew what Maggie was talking about when the older woman urged, 'Come on, Dawn—look!'

'Oh ...' She dragged her attention back reluctantly, and then gave a self-deprecating shrug. 'Who would ...'

'Any one of a dozen young men!' Maggie insisted. 'You know you're the prettiest girl here, and the least they can hope for is a dance. Look!'

Dawn was not at all convinced that anyone would dare defy Byron's claim on her within the ritual of the straws, and besides, the people on the

island seemed too reserved to approach a perfect
stranger with such an intimate custom. But, to
please Maggie, she unfolded her napkin. And to
her very great surprise, a broken piece of straw fell
out. It was dyed berry red, and as she picked it up
her eyes fell automatically on Vernon, gazing with
sweet shyness at her across the lawn. She thought,
Oh, no! Endearing, thoughtful, harmless little
Vernon. What in the world was she to do now?

Maggie was saying, 'Now, remember, the man
can't approach you. You must go to him, and
demand to see his half of the straw. Once you do,
he can't refuse to show it to you. Now, go ahead.'
She gave her an excited little shove. 'Ask around—
find him!'

But Dawn merely clutched the straw in her hand
and thought the best thing to do was to make
herself unobtrusive for a while. She didn't want to
hurt his feelings, but if she caught another glimpse
of those calf-like eyes she might weaken. Of all
things she did not want to start something that
could very easily turn into an awkward situation,
for she must be here another two weeks.

She slipped away from the crowd and wandered
out of the periphery of the celebration towards the
lake. In its dark depths glowed the light of a
hundred torches, flickering and dancing, but silent.
Dawn sat on the grassy bank, enjoying the sounds
of the music and the laughter from a distance, glad,
for the moment not to join it.

Her reflection in the lake gave back a girl she
hardly knew, the long blue dress with its tight
square bustline, the hair almost white in the
moonlight and trailing on the ground, eyes wide
and wistful . . . Like a fanciful painting someone
had made of her. Looking at that reflection, she

allowed herself to dream she *was* a fairy princess, and all the world was at her command. And for her first wish, she would have . . .

She started as a shadow took form over her reflection, thinking for a wild moment of wishes come true, and then Byron sat down beside her. For a time he did not speak, absently plucking little stalks of grass and letting them float down into the lake, and all traces of his former merrymaking good spirits were gone. Then he said, 'Is everything all right?'

She nodded, swallowing hard before she could speak. Each time he was near it was worse . . . 'I'm a little tired, I think. All that noise . . . and excitement . . .'

Byron nodded. 'It will go on until daybreak.'

She looked alarmed, and he smiled. 'Don't worry, we're not expected to stay that long. Go on up any time you want; we all realise you're a working girl.' And then he hesitated, a very slight frown creasing his brow which puzzled Dawn. He asked gently, 'Aren't you having a good time, Dawn?'

'Oh, I am,' she assured him quickly, genuinely. 'I think it's wonderful. It's all so new—and exciting—it makes my head spin.'

He smiled a little, and seemed to relax. His voice was low and touched with a quiet note of sincerity as he answered. 'I wanted you to have a good time. I wanted this night to be special for you.' And then his hand came up to cup her face, the light in his eyes growing and deepening as he looked at her, and her heart leapt in quick anticipation, a rush of joy to know that she could put that look in his eyes. 'You look like a medieval princess sitting here,' he said softly. 'You look the way I've imagined you, so many times, as though you've belonged here for ever . . .'

Her lips parted on a breath, she saw the quickening leap of response in his eyes and she knew he was going to kiss her. She had never wanted anything so badly in her life as she wanted his kiss at that moment.

But Byron dropped his hand, and then his eyes. He turned to look back over the lake. Something changed subtly about him then, and Dawn, aching with confusion and disappointment, could not tell what it was. Sadness, anger, disappointment . . . No, none of those familiar emotions. It was something she had never seen before, but his moods were so varied and so swift it was impossible to analyse them. One moment he was so close he seemed almost a part of her, and in the next he was a remote and distant stranger. Now he seemed to hover somewhere in between, and there was an odd tone to his voice as he said, 'I hope you don't find all our pagan rites and customs too offensive to participate in.'

Quickly, she thought she understood the reason for his sudden coolness, and she hastened to apologise, 'Byron, about what happened before, I didn't mean to embarrass you or insult your custom——'

But he impatiently waved it away. 'That I understand.' And he looked at her, his eyes not angry, merely curious and perhaps—only slightly— hurt. 'But I don't understand what you could find distasteful about our innocent little straw game. How could that have offended you?'

Now she was confused. She did not know what to say, and she could only look at him helplessly.

Byron said abruptly, 'You didn't ask me.'

She caught her breath, hardly daring to believe what he implied. His dark eyes were open and serious, and her heart went into a series of wild, unrestrained acrobatics. Slowly she opened her hand to reveal her straw.

He reached into his pocket and took out the other half, placing it on her palm. And then, very slowly, very tenderly, he took her in his arms.

She kissed him with an openness and a depth of emotion she had never been able to give before, and for a time the lights and the music and the laughter faded around her. There was only the two of them, melting into one, his strong lean fingers pressing into her bare back, her hands against his neck beneath the rough garment, caressing, exploring, inviting more. Then he pushed her away, his breath a little shaky, his eyes raw and hungry. 'My God, girl,' he whispered hoarsely, 'how much more of this do you think I can stand?'

'Oh, Byron, I——'

'Hush!' Swiftly he placed his finger across her lips. 'It's all right. I understand.' He closed his eyes briefly, as though subduing pain, and when he opened them again he pried open her fist and removed the two pieces of straw.

He spoke quietly as his fingers worked nimbly with the straw, and Dawn watched him in silent fascination, loving him, yearning for him. 'You may find our island ways a little wild sometimes, maybe we're too much a world to ourselves. We're not much for culture, or refinement, or all the other things you're probably used to in New York. There are no fancy hotels or theatres, and God willing, there never will be. But I'm not anchored here, you know. I travel a good bit, meeting our buyers and distributors on the Continent, and even in America occasionally. And you still have your work, which will take you about a good bit. With your talent it should be as easy to freelance as to work for a company . . .'

Dawn whispered breathlessly, searching his eyes, 'Byron . . . what are you saying?'

His smile was gentle, though a little rueful, and far beneath the surface was even a hint of uncertainty. 'Perhaps too much,' he admitted. 'I tend to make decisions very quickly and it's presumptuous of me to credit you with the same trait. I'm not trying to rush you, Dawn, love . . .' The softening in his eyes took her breath away, as did the gentle caress of his finger along the side of her face. 'But it's been apparent to me for some time now that this is where you belong, and what I'm offering you now is a chance to think it over . . .'

The emotions that rushed through her and were reflected in her eyes were too rapid and too intense to be catalogued, and once again Byron stopped her from speaking. 'No,' he said quietly, very seriously, 'I don't want impulsive decisions from you. Once . . .' He dropped his eyes, he took her limp hand very lightly in his. 'Once you asked from me promises of permanence and fidelity. I told you one couldn't receive those vows unless one were first prepared to give them. This . . .' his voice was husky as he placed the little ring of interwoven straws on her finger, 'is my pledge to you. All I ask tonight is that you accept it.'

Dawn could not speak. She could not, for a moment, even breathe. She could only stare in amazement and incredible, bubbling joy at the crude ring Byron had placed on her finger until hot tears blurred the night into a kaleidoscope of vibrant, glowing happiness. Perhaps it was only on magical nights such as this that dreams did come true.

She lifted shining eyes to him, and the broken whisper that bubbled from her lips came from the depths of her heart. 'Oh, Byron! I—I love you!'

She saw the quick leap of joy and wonder in his eyes just before her lips met his and she gave to him all herself, all her love, the promise of forever. The night died out about them in spinning colours and echoing delight as their passion built and needs too long denied rose to claim them, and then, at the last possible moment, Byron pushed her away.

She could feel the wild beating of his heart against hers and the unsteadiness of his breath upon her face as he held her for just one more moment. His voice was low and hoarse as he murmured, 'No, love ... you know what you're doing to me. I won't have you until you're sure ...'

And reluctantly, with one more unsteady breath, he drew her to her feet. She was sure, she wanted to tell him so, surely he could see it in her eyes. All she wanted was to be with him, for ever ...

His smile was somewhat strained, the hand which smoothed back her hair had a noticeable tremor to it. And he said huskily, 'Go inside now, to the safety of your room. You have a lot to think about, because I won't accept half-hearted commitments.'

Yes, she had a lot to think about. Her head was spinning with it as she walked alone back to her room, seeking privacy, a quiet place to come to some sort of acceptance of what had just happened to her ... a dream come true. He wanted her to stay with him. He wanted her for his wife ... she was to live here in the Hebrides, mistress of this lsland, with the only man she had ever loved as her partner ... It was a lot to think about, but at the same time, hardly anything at all. It was simply all she had ever wanted, all her life, and what was there to decide?

She lay awake in her bed for hours, hearing the revelry at last die down below, watching the moon rise over her window, too excited, too filled with promise to sleep. Why had he made her wait? She did not want to wait, she wanted to be with him, to share her love with him tonight and always ...

She got out of bed in her nightgown and crossed the room. A few steps would put her in Byron's arms, where she had always belonged ...

She opened the door, and heard soft footsteps on the carpeted corridor. That was better, he was only now coming to bed and he would see her ... she would go to him ... and then, only then, would it all be as she had dreamed.

He rounded the corner, and he was not alone. His arm was around Hilary's waist, his head bent close to hers, and they were smiling with the secret only lovers share. Numbly, Dawn watched him open the door to one of the bedrooms and follow her inside.

She went back to her own bed, shaken and cold. And though she lay there, dry-eyed and devastated, listening throughout the night, she never heard them leave the room.

CHAPTER NINE

DAWN was up early the next morning, not having slept at all, and had packed and dressed before even the first sounds began to stir from the kitchen. The first ferry to Oban left at ten o'clock and she intended to be on it.

On her dressing-table lay the little ring of woven straws . . . what, a joke? A passing fantasy? Or perhaps only another attempt at seduction which, when rebuffed, had finally convinced Byron she was not worth the trouble. Not when Hilary, so familiar, so inviting in her see-through gown, so very willing, was only an arm's reach away . . . She remembered from long ago Maggie's words, 'There are some things Byron simply cannot forgive . . .'

Well, she thought, lifting her chin and swallowing hard against the burning lump in her throat which had lodged there all night and would not break away, there are some things I simply cannot forgive, either.

Through the night, refusing to give way to tears, she had managed to become very hard, to reach a safe distance from which to view the entire situation. She would not admit, even to herself, the wrenching pain Byron had caused her, the awful, devastating hurt. Anger, she would confess, scorn at herself for being so vulnerable, but he would never know how effectively his betrayal had cut her. If he had intended to hurt her, he would be disappointed. She would not fling accusations in his face, she would not lower herself to pleas of fidelity and broken promises. If he could make those promises in such a terse, logical way, and then turn so casually to the bed of another woman, she could be just as cool. She could play his sophisticated games.

So at nine o'clock she applied a heavy coat of make-up to disguise her pale, drawn face, gathered up her luggage and her camera bag, placed a bright, frozen smile on her face, and went downstairs.

Byron came out of the dining room as she was getting out of the elevator. Her heart lurched and twisted at the sight of him, so fresh and well rested, so utterly casual in a pair of tight jeans and a creamy cable-knit sweater, his hands extended, a smile on his face. Dawn realised how seldom he smiled, how often she had longed for a smile to break across those stormy features, and now, when it no longer mattered, he was the way she would want to remember him—relaxed, happy, smiling.

'Well,' he said, coming towards her, 'I expected you down long before this! What would you like to do today, my love?' And suddeny his eyes fell on the luggage she was unloading from the lift, the smile disappeared into curiosity. 'What is this?'

She placed her camera bag on top of the suitcase and took one steadying breath before turning to him with that painted smile. 'I'll tell you, Byron,' she responded pleasantly, 'I was thinking about what you said yesterday, and I do believe it would be easiser to base myself at Oban. Not that I haven't appreciated your hospitality, you understand, but it just wouldn't be convenient for me to stay here any longer.'

There was confusion on his face, and disbelief, and a twinge of uncertain amusement as he came towards her. Apparently he thought she was not serious. 'Don't be daft, love, you know I was only joking. Now, what's all the luggage for?'

'Yes,' she replied evenly. 'I know you were only joking.' About everything. She could not resist that one stab. How could he face her so innocently? What kind of man was he that he could deceive so easily without one twinge of conscience?

He scowled. 'You'll find out sooner or later that I'm not known for my patience, and I really don't feel like sparring with you this morning. Now just what,' he demanded, 'do you think you're doing?'

She resumed her bright façade. 'I think,' she replied, 'I'm going to catch the ten o'clock ferry to Oban, where I'll finish my assignment and be back in New York before the month is out. Now, I really don't want to walk carrying all this luggage, so if I could impose upon you for the use of your car one more time . . .'

She thought his swarthy face might have paled a shade as he stared at her in patent shock and disbelief. Almost, seeing him like that, her own reserve broke, almost she gave way to her own hurt and disillusionment and screamed the ugly truth to him. Almost she would have forgiven him if he had given her a chance.

But he continued to deny it. 'Oban . . . New York . . . *What are you talking about?* What's going on with you? Last night——'

She laughed lightly, bitterly. 'Oh, Byron, really!' There, just the right touch of flirtatious sophistication. Just what he had always expected of her. Exactly what he had wanted. 'It was great fun while it lasted, but we both knew we weren't playing for keeps, didn't we? A day, two weeks . . .' she shrugged. 'What difference does it make.'

'You said,' he accused, 'you would stay!'

And you said, she thought angrily, and almost lost that precious, cool, life-preserving composure, *For ever!* But no, he had not ever really said it. He had been very careful not to use that word.

'Come on, Byron,' she managed, though in a slightly tinny voice, 'come off the games, already! Like I said, it's been fun, but . . .' she shrugged and smiled brightly, 'the world beckons! I've got things to do, places to see, and . . .' she glanced at her watch, 'if I don't hurry I'm going to miss the boat! So, if you wouldn't mind, the car . . .'

In two swift steps he was beside her, his grip so painful on her arm that she almost cried out, his face black and stormy above hers. *'What the hell,'* he hissed, *'kind of woman are you?'*

Her bright façade broke under his unjustified wrath, all the anger and hurt of betrayal was written in her eyes, but she would not cry. She would not let him know. She said coldly, 'Let go of my arm.'

For a moment longer he looked at her, loathing, contemptuous, and, yes—faint, but there—hurt. Then he released her so forcefully that she had to fling out her hand to keep from falling over her luggage, and he stalked away.

Shaking, Dawn stood there a moment longer, trying to find the courage to meet the next half hour before Falkone's Acres, with all its hurt and longing and heartbreak, would be out of her life for ever. Then, sternly, she pulled herself together and went to find Maggie.

'Leaving?' Maggie exclaimed incredulously when Dawn told her. 'But I thought it was all arranged. You were going to stay here, and—whatever you need, I'm sure we can work it out . . .'

Not this, thought Dawn. No one can work this out. 'No,' she explained patiently. It was a lot harder to keep up the front with Maggie than it had been with Byron. She was emotionally exhausted. 'It really just wouldn't work out. I've got to get this assignment in and be back in New York, and time is important. It will be much easier for me from Oban.'

'But today?' Maggie insisted. 'Must you leave today?'

'I'm afraid so.' The muscles of her face were beginning to ache from the effort of maintaining that pleasant smile. 'Like I said, time . . .'

Maggie's disappointment was undisguised. 'What a shame! I was hoping . . .' She caught herself in a faraway look, and shook her head sadly. 'Never mind what I was hoping. If you must leave today, I'll drive you down to the dock. Are you all packed?'

'Yes, but I don't want to take you away . . .' The castle was coming to life with the activity of those hired to clean up after the party, a dozen girls inside, a score of workmen and gardeners outside, dismantling tables and repairing the damage the festivities had done to the lawn. Maggie was busy and could not be spared, but that was not the real reason Dawn did not want her to go with her. She preferred to say her goodbyes to the castle and everything connected with it here.

'Nonsense,' answered Maggie, going for her keys. She glanced at her one last time. 'I just wish you would reconsider . . .'

Dawn shook her head, once, firmly.

The ferry was already boarding as they arrived, and that was best. It meant no time for long goodbyes.

'Now are you sure,' offered Maggie, 'that you

don't want me to drive you? It will be a lot easier, finding a hotel.'

'No, I can take a cab.' She passed the last of her luggage to the captain's assistant, who carried it on board, and then she paused at Maggie's window, smiling with genuine regret. 'Well,' she said, 'thanks for everything.'

'It's been our pleasure, Dawn,' she replied sincerely. 'Remember, we open the first of next month. Maybe . . . maybe you'll come and visit us again.'

Her smile faded into vague sadness. Maybe, years from now, she would come back, alone, as a guest, and remember a time when a young girl very much like her had learned a lot about love and life beneath the ancient walls of the castle.

The warning horn blew deafeningly loud in her ears, and she was glad to have to hurry. 'Goodbye!' Maggie called, and she waved back to her as she ran quickly up the boarding steps.

The ferry was not very crowded that morning; few of the islanders had yet recovered from last night's revelry, and, as it was Saturday, there was little transaction with the mainland. There were two or three cars, and perhaps half a dozen passengers on foot. As she moved towards the back to stand with the other passengers, she was surprised to see the door of a little red M.G. open, and hear someone call her name.

It was Hilary, uncurling her long legs from their small confine, tying a green print chiffon scarf over her hair as she rose and came towards her. 'Hello,' she called over the noise of the motor. 'I didn't expect to see you here.'

Of all people, Dawn had not expected to meet her. Over and over the scene played in her mind—

Hilary's arm about Byron, her provocative gown clinging to her body, going into the bedroom . . . But the anger she felt was not towards Hilary, the pain was not because of her. It could be expected of her. All was fair in love and war . . .

The smell of diesel engines and salt water was lost in the subtle, alluring scent she wore as Hilary came to stand beside her. 'You're not leaving, are you?'

'Yes,' Dawn replied stiffly, turning to look out over the rail. 'I have another assignment.'

'Imagine that,' drawled Hilary, and with a great effort Dawn restrained herself from turning to look at her face. 'And I thought . . .' She laughed lightly. 'Well, it just goes to show you, doesn't it?' She came to lean on the rail beside Dawn, and at that moment the spires and towers of Falkone's Acres floated into view over the misty treetops. Her last view of it wrenched painfully at her heart. 'Pretty, isn't it?' said Hilary. 'Really makes you sad to leave.'

Dawn could not help turning to stare at her. 'Leave? You're leaving?'

'Oh, yes,' Hilary replied. 'I'm moving to the mainland. Of course it's not as though I'll never be back—for a visit now and then, perhaps—but life on an island can get to be rather of a bore, you know.'

After last night . . . and she was leaving! What had it been, then—for old times' sake? Or was that the way people like Byron and Hilary preferred it, a series of one-night stands, no ties, no promises. She shuddered at the sudden thought that if she had stayed, unaware, and married Byron, every time Hilary came back for those 'visits' there would have been more of the same . . .

Hilary glanced at her through narrowed, sea-darkened eyes. 'Did you hear? Byron decided to forgive me, after all.' She laughed lightly, straightening up. 'I knew he would. He's too smart a man to let something like this ruin his business.' She started to wander away, then glanced back. 'If you need a lift at Oban, just let me know.'

Dawn only shook her head numbly, too shocked to speak.

Yes, she had learned a lot about love and life at Falkone's Acres.

She checked into a small hotel near the waterfront at Oban. From her window she could watch the dingy little fishing boats leave every morning and look out over the pier as their hauls were brought in at night. Her room was cramped, though clean and rather quaint. It was nothing like the splendour she had enjoyed at the castle.

Almost, as she sat at the window and looked out over the clear sea, she could imagine she saw the point of a lush green island bobbing up and down among the waves. Almost, if she closed her eyes, she could see a majestic tower of stones rising above the trees ...

She did not go out that day. She broke down and let herself cry.

She filled the days from first light until dusk travelling about the islands, using the ferry for major excursions, going on foot or by pony around the rugged mountain cliffs, looking for something worth photographing. At any other time it would have been an exciting, adventure-filled time of her life, she would have seen magic in every crevice and corner and captured it on film. She would have seen character in the craggy face of a peasant farmer, simplicity in a children's game, beauty in the slim bodies of the island girls. All she saw was endless green meadows, dirty brown sheep, flat lakes and foreboding mountains. She took her pictures, but nothing which might have been better portrayed on the back of a postcard. The islands were all the same, each thatched cottage very much like the next, and not one of the farmers, all placidly tilling their rows, was after all very different from another.

In the middle of the week she called her editor long-distance. 'Look,' she said, 'this thing is just not working out. All I've got is a bunch of junk. Is it O.K. if I wind this thing up and catch a plane home this weekend?'

The silence on the other end reflected surprise. 'What's the matter?' he taunted. 'Homesick? Or just can't take the pressure?'

'Pressure!' she laughed mirthlessly. 'This place is as dead as a tomb. Really, Joe, there's nothing to shoot.'

'I don't understand,' he objected. '*How* can there be nothing to shoot? The stuff I got on Falkone's Acres was terrific. You were on a roll. What happened?'

Dawn hesitated, then sighed. 'Maybe that's what happened. I peaked too soon. Anyway, I've got some stuff you can use as background if you want, but I'm afraid what you already have is the best you're going to see. I'm just wasting your money staying here.'

Another pause. 'I'm disappointed in you, Dawn.'

She didn't care. She almost said it out loud.

'All right, then,' he said at last, 'do what you have to. We reserved the whole next issue for you, you know that? The people in layout are going to be plenty mad!'

The phone call had depressed her, for more than the obvious reasons. It brought back too poignantly the reality of New York, back to the darkroom to wait for another chance which might not be so soon in coming this time—her bright little apartment with its chic furnishings, plants which needed to be watered, dinners for one, her temperamental grey cat now in the custody of a girlfriend, the endless round of dates, hoping that each one would be that one, very special man ... And it never was.

The grey, misty day was no consolation. She could not sit at her window and stare at it all day, but she did not feel like donning her outdoor togs and braving the weather for a few more dull photographs. She decided to go down to the small dining room for a cup of tea.

It was empty, and the girl who served her obviously resented her midday break being interrupted. She sat at the window and once again looked out on to a relentless day, trying to remember if life had ever looked so bleak from her tower room at Falkone's Acres.

Then, in the midst of her reverie, there was a voice, startling her so in its familiarity that she spilled some of the tea on to the saucer as she turned.

'Dawn! How perfectly lovely! You know, I thought I might run into you here, this being the only decent hotel in town.' It was Maggie, slipping off a grey wool coat as she crossed the small room with purposeful, clicking steps on the linoleum. 'As a matter of fact,' she confided, as she slipped into the chair across the table from her, 'I was going to look you up before I left. I just had to see how you were getting on.' She clasped her free hand on the table warmly. 'And how are you?'

Dawn was flooded with relief to see again her strong square face with its boyish cut of grey hair, to clasp her firm brown hand which brought back memories of good times, warmth, and—home. Maggie had become like a mother to her, or an older sister, and she had not realised before how sad she would be not to see her again. But mostly she brought back memories of Byron, in those good times when her days were filled with hope, and the wonder of discovering love.

'It's good to see you,' she beamed. 'I never thought we'd meet again!' And then her gratification faded into something more intense, like trepidation mixed with dreadful excitement. 'Is Byron——?'

'Oh, no,' Maggie said briskly, with a dismissing wave of her hand. 'I'm here for Hilary, you know, and even the *most* broadminded person couldn't expect him to come—despite the changes!' There were several points in that simple sentence which Dawn would have liked cleared up, but Maggie continued without giving her a chance. 'But you didn't tell me. How are you doing here? About ready to reconsider and come back to the island for a while?'

Dawn shook her head, trying to maintain a smile even though she lost eye contact. 'As a matter of fact, this whole idea isn't working out too well. I'm going home this weekend.'

'What a shame!' Then Maggie made a very astute statement. 'I suppose once you've seen Falkone's Acres nothing can compare, can it?'

'Yes,' Dawn agreed. 'That's right.' Then, as conversation lapsed, she said, 'You mentioned you were here because of Hilary. I met her on the ferry coming over, but she didn't mention . . .'

'Her wedding,' explained Maggie. 'Didn't you know?'

Wedding! But only moments ago Maggie had said Byron was not here, was not expected . . . Her wedding!

'But then,' Maggie was continuing, 'how could you know, if no one ever mentioned it to you? It's going to be a quiet little affair here in Oban, but I felt as though *someone* should come to represent the family, especially since we're going to try to keep up good relations with the Manns. Naturally, it was out of the question for Byron to come, so I was elected. I don't particularly care for the girl myself . . .' she shrugged, 'but I have nothing against her father, and we can't let this feud drag on for ever . . .'

Dawn had to interrupt, though she knew her question was stupid, even to her own ears, and so was her numb tone of voice. 'But—I thought Hilary was going to marry Byron.'

Maggie stared at her. 'My dear, I thought I explained all that to you! Yes, I know I did. She's marrying that young man from Mountain Distilleries—Russell Douglas! Yes, I'm sure I made that clear . . .' she frowned, and then suddenly her brow cleared with an exclamation. 'Unless you thought there'd been a reconciliation between Hilary and Byron!'

Dawn flushed, but would not reveal to Maggie what she knew. There was no need to hurt this kind woman with it, and one did not go carrying tales to the maligner's sister, and it was simple pride which would force her to keep her counsel. Above all, she did not want anyone feeling sorry for her. So she only defended, 'Hilary did— mention something about—a reconciliation on the ferry.'

'Oh!' There was relief in Maggie's laughter. 'For a moment I thought you might have got the wrong impression, and that was why you left ... No,' she explained, 'Hilary must have been referring to the *business* reconciliation, which we were all glad to see happen!'

Dawn supposed that, after having slept with the daughter, Byron could hardly hold a grudge against her father. Yes, she had supported a reconciliation, too, but not on those terms.

Suddenly Maggie became serious, and she lowered her tone a fraction. Dawn thought that perhaps this was the closest she would ever come to seeing that stern woman look uncomfortable. 'Dawn,' she said in a moment, glancing down at the tablecloth, and then up again, 'do you mind if I speak with you about something—personal?'

Dawn shook her head, and could not imagine what she could be referring to. 'No, of course not. Go ahead.'

Maggie leaned forward, clasping her hands on the table. 'You came to mean a great deal—to us all—while you were at Falkone's Acres. You changed our lives, in a way. You were able to get to Byron when no one else could. First, it was his attitude about opening the castle, and then ... well, I hold you entirely responsible for the continuance of the partnership.' Dawn looked surprised, but she went on, 'I think—it was through you that he found the grace to forgive Hilary, and because of you he found his perspective on the entire situation. Now, Dawn,' she took a breath, 'I know I'm speaking out of turn, meddling in my brother's affairs, and getting very personal. But he was in love with you, Dawn.'

She turned her face away quickly, so that the

other woman might not see the pain which streaked across it. She did not want to hear. It was over, if it had ever really been, and Maggie did not know how cruel she was being by bringing it all up again.

But she continued imperviously, 'I've never seen him—as affected by anyone as he was by you. I've never seen him change so. And I know you felt the same way about him because ...' She took another breath. 'Well, because I'm a woman, and I just know.'

Dawn managed, 'Please, Maggie ...'

But that would not do. She insisted, 'The darkroom. Do you really think he had it installed for only that one use? No, it was for you, because he knew—he thought—you would stay. And getting you those extra two weeks in the islands— oh, yes, I know all about that! Did you know you could get married in two weeks with a special licence?'

Now Dawn turned to look at her, shock and incredulity and pain bare on her face. And her mind kept echoing, Even then ... even then, before he said a word to me, before I guessed ... It was with a strange spiralling mixture of pain and joy as she realised that even then he had loved her as she had loved him. But then it was an abrupt downward plunge as she remembered what had happened between then and now. And no, not love. He had never said a word about love.

She managed, in a remarkably even tone, 'Maggie, you shouldn't be telling me these things.'

'I know,' Maggie admitted miserably. 'And I'm the worst sort of woman for doing it, but I couldn't let you go—without knowing! I swear to you, Dawn, he's my brother and I know him, and

I've never known him feel for a woman the way he
felt for you. Hilary . . .' She gave a negligent turn
of her wrist. 'They grew up together; they were old
friends; it was expected. There was no—excitement
there. She never caused him to change. And,
except for the anger, it was no great loss to him
when she left. But you . . .' She closed her eyes
briefly. 'You can't imagine what he's been like
since you left. You see, he took a great risk with
you, and Byron is not known for taking risks. All
this in two weeks—he's never been impulsive
before, but he was that sure of you, of what he felt
for you, and in a simple matter of a fortnight he
knew he wanted you for his wife. When you left,
he lost heavily. He's been—I can't explain it—like
a madman. First Hilary, which was simply a
matter of principle, and then you—a matter of the
heart. It's almost more than I could expect him to
stand.'

Dawn did not know what to say. Her hands,
clasped tightly together under the table, were
shaking, and the tremors were beginning to creep
up her arms. She could not tell Maggie why, but
she could not except any of what she was saying.
No matter how much she wanted to.

Maggie said, 'If only you'd come back with
me . . . I know something must have happened
between the two of you, some misunderstanding,
and if only you would see him once more, I'm
certain it could all be cleared up.'

Dawn shook her head firmly, automatically.
'No—misunderstanding. Nothing that could be
cleared up.' But if there were a magic wand
someone could wave in the air and take back the
night of the festival when two people had walked
into a room and not come out . . . If there were

some potion someone could sprinkle over her to make her forget, if only she could find a way to forgive that one failing, that one broken promise . . .

But it was the most important promise of all.

'Oh, there you are.' They looked up to see Thomas Mann coming towards them, smiling pleasantly at Maggie. 'I thought perhaps you'd gone up to your room.'

Although Maggie obviously resented the interruption, she hid it with grace. 'Thomas, you remember Miss Morrison? Thomas came over on the ferry with me. We'll be going back right after the ceremony.'

'Of course I remember Miss Morrison!' He bent over her hand and Dawn invited him to be seated. 'This,' he smiled to Maggie as he pulled up a chair, 'is the young lady to whom you were telling me we owe all our good fortune.' He looked at her. 'I'm glad to have the opportunity to thank you.'

Dawn smiled stiffly, her head still reeling with the new discoveries Maggie had unleashed about Byron, her chest still aching with the awful pain. And now she must sit and be polite to this veritable stranger, and pretend that nothing was amiss. She said, 'I think Maggie is exaggerating. All I did was express an opinion, and it was the same one I'm sure Byron had heard many times before. I'm glad to see that he made the right decision.'

He said, 'We all are. Oh, it's not as though I would have missed the money, you understand—in fact, it would have been Byron who would have taken the loss. But I've grown to love the place, and I have a real personal feeling for the business, and I would have missed it. It would have been a great shame to see an old friendship and a good partnership break up over something like that.'

Again, Dawn smiled politely.

He chuckled. 'He kept me hanging on until the last minute, though, that he did. He had me waiting in the office, wearing out the carpet, on the night of the festival—that's when the contract was due to expire, you know, at midnight that night. And I do swear, it was on the very stroke of midnight that he walked in with Hilary, just as casual as you please, and announced that we hadn't much to negotiate, after all . . .'

Dawn looked up. 'Midnight? The night of the festival?' Her heart was beginning to pound with an awful fear. Perhaps she had misunderstood. Surely, dear heavens, she had not heard correctly? She had to say it. 'But I saw Byron about that time, and he was nowhere near the office.'

He looked confused, as though wondering what possible difference Byron's whereabouts at that particular hour could make to her. She had spoiled his story. Then he said, 'Oh, you must mean the lower-floor office. Goodness me, no, with all that racket going on down there we couldn't have heard ourselves think! No, we used his private study, on the upper floor. That must have been where you saw him.'

Dawn went pale, and the back of her mind picked up on his jocular words as he continued with his story, 'I don't believe any of us left that room before the crack of dawn, talking and celebrating . . . just like old times. Yes, it was, just like old times . . .'

Dawn felt limp, wrung out, totally incapable of movement or speech or even thought. And her mind kept echoing, Oh no, oh no . . . *What had she done?*

Two old friends, apologising after an argument, with their arms about one another. Byron could never say anything without touching; it was his way, it did not necessarily mean what it could appear to. It was her wretched suspicious mind, her refusal to trust anyone, which had turned an innocent office into a bedroom, a business meeting into an assignation. No need now to try to justify it, no need to think rationalisation could make it different, for she had done it, it was unforgivable, but she had done it, sacrificed the man she loved and the entire rest of her life to one insane, jealous moment.

And Byron. Oh, Byron ... What must he be thinking of her now? The darkroom, the scheme with her editor, a little ring woven of straws ... And she was gone without explanation or apology. How hateful she had been that last morning! How unfeeling, in her own imagined pain, to his hurt. She could not think of the role she had acted on that day without a bitter taste rising to her mouth. But over that was the astonishment and confusion on Byron's face—she had mistaken it for a disgusting sophistication, and in fact it was genuine innocence. What did he think of her? Exactly what she had wanted him to think, that she was as heartless and flirtatious as she had imagined him to be, that all along she had been playing a game while he was deadly serious. And how she had wronged him!

She did not think she could ever face him again, but she knew she must. She knew he did not want her, and rejection, above all things, was what she had throughout her life most feared. But she must somehow find the courage to face him, and to give him an explanation. It was a shameful, implausible, inexcusable explanation, but it must be done.

'Maggie.' She did not realise she had interrupted a conversation until they both turned to look at her. 'I was thinking ... did you say you were going back tonight?'

'That's right,' answered Maggie curiously.

She glanced down at her hands in her lap which, when she unclasped them, bore red marks from the imprint of her fingers. 'Well——' she took a breath, and tried to force casualness into her tone, 'I was thinking. There are a few more shots of the island I'd like to get, and the forecast is clear for tomorrow. Do you think I could go back with you, after all?'

The relief that spread over Maggie's face was wonderful to see. 'Of course! Of course you can!'

Dawn did not try to deceive herself into thinking she would find that same welcome on Byron's face.

CHAPTER TEN

DAWN took only an overnight bag, and when they arrived at the island just before ten o'clock she said a quiet goodnight to Maggie and crept upstairs to her room like a thief. There was no sign of Byron, and if she could postpone it only for a few more hours, if she could wait until morning to confront him, maybe her sinking courage would be restored.

She was swept by pathos as she entered the room which felt like home to her. Here she had lain so many nights dreaming of a dark, impenetrable man of unbounded passions and unimagined depth. She walked over to the window where once she had leaned out and heard a serenade, looked over the garden with hot memories of unbridled lust and a near escape. She turned back into the room and began to undress slowly. And here, in this room, she had opened the door and seen Byron with another woman, here she had lain awake until dawn, listening, torturing herself with dark imaginings . . .

She was foolish to have come. How could she face the hurt and accusation in his eyes again? What could she say to him? How could she ask him to forgive her for something for which she could not even forgive herself?

She drew a filmy blue robe over her slip and sat down to unpin her hair. She could not go to bed just yet.

The door opened suddenly and she whirled with a little gasp of alarm, drawing the inadequate bit of nylon together over her slip, letting the hairpins drop from her fingers. Byron stood there, his face dark and forbidding, and she cried, 'Don't you knock?' before she realised that was not the way she had meant to begin this unwanted interview.

Byron stepped inside, but left the door open behind him. 'Maggie told me you were here,' he said. 'But I had to see for myself.' His lips twisted into a slight sneer. 'Come back for more of the same, my dear? Fun and games? Well, perhaps you won't like playing by *my* rules for a change!'

She rose to meet him, every muscle in her body quivering, but she hid it effectively. She said calmly, 'I came to explain.'

'Explain?' He wandered over to the dressing table, moving like a graceful, powerful animal in his black denim jacket and white shirt, standing only inches from her now as he casually lifted her hairbrush, examined it a moment, then set it down again. His voice was deceptively, almost frighteningly, mild. 'I wasn't aware that any explanations were due. I thought you made yourself abundantly clear the morning you left.'

Dawn took a breath, and when she turned to face him she had to take a step backwards for his alarming nearness. 'Byron, I don't blame you for feeling the way you do . . .'

He gave a short, ugly bark of laughter. 'How very generous of you! Oh, yes, my love, I discover new and delightful things about you every day. First it's merely that you're a flirt and a tease, then that you're a first-class actress and tremendous liar, and now, that you possess a heart that's as generous as your little mind is devious!' He flung himself into a chair and fastened a menacing, glittering gaze on her. 'Pray, enlighten me further!

One day I shall be able to boast that I've been had by a mistress of the art, and I wouldn't want to overlook any of the intriguing details of your sordid little character!'

She felt her cheeks begin to tingle beneath the lashing, but she would not buckle. She deserved the worst he was thinking, and more. If only once, she thought a little desperately, he had been gentle with me. If only once I'd known that kindness from him that I could try to latch on to, and discover again ... perhaps this wouldn't be so hopeless. But now whatever passion he had felt for her had turned to hatred, and there was no way to reach him, no way at all. Only honour demanded that she try.

She said swiftly, 'Byron, I came to apologise.'

He lifted an eyebrow with infuriating mockery. 'Now, that's a new twist. Very well, I'm intrigued. Apologise. Let's begin with the first time you came on to me, there in the woods on the day you arrived . . .'

That was too much. 'How can you say that?' she cried. 'You know I didn't——'

A cool tilt of his head, and she knew he had baited her. 'Very well,' he continued with a dismissing flick of his wrist. 'Your conscience won't take you back *that* far, I see. Let's skip right over the many times you lured me to the brink of your bed and then slammed the door in my face. Let's not mention the night you lay in my arms and whispered tearful words about "promises" and "for ever". Would you like to talk about what you did when you finally tricked me into offering those promises? Now *that* should be interesting!'

Hot tears stung her eyes and she blinked them away. 'I did *not* trick you!'

He folded his arms, sat back and waited.

Dawn continued shakily, 'I—never tried to trick you. I—never wanted anything from you but what you were willing to give, freely——'

Byron laughed harshly. 'That's priceless!' Suddeny he stood and crossed the room to the window. 'That is really priceless, because I told myself the same thing about you. But there are many ways a woman can use a man, my dear, and you know them all. Even now . . .' he turned with a sharp gesture towards her, 'you can't resist standing there half dressed, tempting me with that incredibly sensuous little body of yours, hoping— what? That for once I'll take you whether you're willing to give or not? That my honour will have flown the same course as yours?' His eyes raked her bitterly up and down. 'That would be your final power over me, wouldn't it? And *that*'s why you've come back! Well, my love . . .' with a violent gesture, he moved past her towards the door, 'that's one trap into which I refuse to step.'

'Byron, wait!'

To her surprise, he turned, his eyes lashing fury, and involuntarily she shrank back. He had her where he wanted her, humiliated, broken, defenceless. And she could not protest any of it. Still, she made a feeble try. 'I'm only—dressed this way because you burst in here without knocking, and— and I'll change if you want, only give me a chance to talk to you!'

He leaned against the wall, folding his arms and crossing his legs at the ankles, fixing a mirthless smile on his features. 'That should be interesting,' he said. 'The changing process, not the conversation. I really can't imagine that you could have anything left to say to me which could possibly hold my attention for more than a few seconds at the outside. I've heard it all.'

She turned away and pressed her hands to her face to try to forcefully push back tears, all but defeated. 'I never imagined you would make this easy for me,' she managed thickly, at last. 'But once—you trusted me enough to ask me to be your wife. Isn't there—enough of that left for you to give me a few more minutes . . . to explain . . .'

'Trust,' Byron said softly, after a moment. 'Now there's a word that interests me. Very often misused, very often misplaced. Very well. Go on, I'm listening.'

But Dawn found, after all, that she could not look at him. She twisted her hands together before her, and in the window she could see her own reflection in the bright lamplight. Her face was white and drawn, one side of her hair released, the other still held by pins. Her white lace slip was only partially covered by the flowing robe, and her chest, bared by the parting of the robe at the throat, was rapidly rising and falling with the tightness of her breath. Over her shoulder was Byron, still lounging against the wall in his black-and-white elegance, waiting.

She said in a small voice, 'That night . . . of the festival—I could hardly believe it when you said— what you did. You were so—matter-of-fact, and— you never mentioned one word about—love.' In the window, she saw him scowl. He uncrossed his ankles and stood up straighter, poised, waiting.

'I never expected it, you see,' she continued, and found the courage to turn to face him. 'I thought you were only amusing yourself——'

'You thought *I*——!' he interrupted in incredulous anger, but she held up a hand in a weak plea for silence.

'And then, later, that night ...' This was the worst part. The awful, humiliating part when she must admit to him her foolishness, her rashness of assumption, her suspicious nature. She finished in a rush, 'I saw you and Hilary come upstairs and go into one of the bedrooms and I thought ... I thought ...'

Slowly, understanding dawned in his face. Understanding and amazement and swift anger. 'You thought I went from you to *her*?'

Before she could answer he was beside her, grasping her wrist with a force that made her cry out in alarm. He half pulled, half dragged her across the room and through the door, down the corridor a few steps to another door, which he flung open, shoving her inside. His hand hit the wall with a reverberating force and the little room sprang into brilliant light. 'Is this it?' he demanded. 'Is this the *bedroom* you saw me enter with Hilary?'

She stood there, blinking in the sudden light, shaking and unable to protest, at that moment, that there was no need for him to show her. It was a small room, strictly utilitarian, crowded with a desk, a bookshelf and filing cabinets. Not even a sofa or a divan to relieve its spartan décor. 'Oh yes,' Byron continued sarcastically, 'it was a night of unforgettable passion—if one is prepared to overlook the fact that that stone floor was uncommonly cold, and Thomas Mann stood over my shoulder every moment, pestering me about contracts ... Dawn Morrison, you're a fool!'

It was more than she could bear, the disgust in his voice, the unvarnished evidence of her cruel mistake confronting her on every side. 'I know,' she whispered, pressing her knuckles to one cheek to staunch the trickle of a tear there. 'I know . . .'

But at last she had to look up at him, and the regret and disappointment in his face was worse, a thousand times worse, than his anger or sarcasm had been. 'I never expected this of you, Dawn,' he said quietly, and turned and left her.

After a long time, she found the strength in her legs to cross the corridor and go back to her room, where she got into bed without undressing and cried herself to sleep.

'There are some things Byron simply can't forgive . . .' The words kept echoing in her mind. She knew it, she had always known it, yet why did she perversely insist upon hoping that this might not be one of them? As she came down the next morning her eyes caught upon the crest gleaming in the sunlight on the foyer wall, and with a sinking heart she knew the ultimate answer to her question. Five centuries of Boyds had built an empire based on trust; why should she expect that motto to be overlooked now simply for her?

'Dawn!'

She turned at the unexpected sound of a familiar voice, and it was Vernon, as bright and cheerful as ever, coming towards her. 'I heard you'd left. What a nice surprise!'

'I did,' she replied, returning his smile weakly. 'I'm only back for—a little while.' She gestured to the camera bag over her shoulder. 'I really hadn't finished here, and the weather looked so nice I thought I'd get my last few shots this morning.'

Byron glanced through the window at the hazy blue sky. 'Looks are deceiving,' he told her. 'There's a mist moving in from the sea. You'd

better hurry if you don't want your lenses to get all
fogged up.'

She smiled a little in acknowledgement, and for
a moment they stood there in an uncomfortable
silence. Then he lifted his briefcase and said, 'I just
came over to pick up some papers. I've really got
to get going.' He paused. 'I guess we won't see
each other again.'

'I guess not,' she agreed, and there was a slight
constriction in her throat. This time the goodbyes
would be permanent, all around.

They both looked towards the tower staircase as
the door opened and Byron came down. He
hesitated, looking at them, and Vernon broke the
tense silence with a cheerful, 'On my way!' And,
over his shoulder to Dawn, casually, 'Goodbye,
then.'

Dawn responded, 'Goodbye,' and was left alone
in the foyer with Byron.

She had not expected to see him this morning,
and she was unprepared for another encounter. Her
heart was wrenched with pain as she looked at
him, so very much like he had been that first day
she had met him, dressed in tight, faded jeans, and
a dark turtleneck sweater, aloof and in control.
With a pang she realised he had not lost his
physical attraction to her, and wondered if he ever
would.

She spoke quickly, before he could, 'As long as I
was here, I thought I'd finish up the article. I'll
leave on the next ferry.'

He nodded, once. 'Do you need the car?'

'No . . . I think I can walk.'

Byron moved past her to take his jacket from
the rack near the door, then he paused. She waited
for him to speak, and it seemed she waited a long

time. At last he said, very quietly, and without
turning, 'I told you once that the only way to
obtain loyalty from another was to first be able to
give your trust. That's—just too important to me.
I can't live without trust. I'm sorry, Dawn.'

She nodded, though he could not see, and
swallowed hard against a new lump that was
forming in her throat. 'I understand,' she
whispered.

It only seemed to her that love would be able to
make allowances for mistakes, to somehow find
forgiveness where before there had been none.

He pulled on his jacket, opening the door, and
was gone.

It was a longer walk to the construction site
than she had imagined, but she did not mind.
Putting one foot in front of the other gave her
something to do, concentrating on reaching her
destination kept her mind busy, so that she could
not dwell upon grief. It was inevitable, after all.
For a brief time she had belonged here, she had
fallen in love here, and perhaps a part of her
would always belong here. But she had a life on
the other side of the world, and it was that to
which she must return. Byron was right, of course.
There must be more than what they had been able
to offer one another. Too many unspoken
promises lay between them.

True to Vernon's prediction, the sky began to
lower as she reached the construction site, and
already the crews were beginning to break up in
anticipation of a downpour. She snapped the
shutter quickly from many angles, watched the
men park their equipment and get into their jeeps,
and then she had an idea for the perfect closing
shot.

There was a rocky overhang a few hundred yards away, near the beach, which did not look too difficult to climb. The vantage point from its summit, overlooking the deserted building site and the stormy sea, would provide the ideal ending to her pictorial story. She was depicting five hundred years of history on Falkone's Acres, and this would be the promise of the future . . . arrested in progress, waiting for what tomorrow might bring.

The climb was somewhat more strenuous than she had anticipated. She scuffed her boots and scraped her hands once or twice, and was hot and out of breath by the time she reached the top. Already the mist was beginning to fall, making the loose shale under her feet slippery and treacherous, but she could retouch the photograph so that the scene would not look too desolate. She took several shots, and it was perfect. As a last sentimental gesture, she swung around and captured the misty mountains, the lofty trees, the moody sea with its single lone fisherman casting and reeling in the surf . . .

She stopped and lowered the camera, watching him as he moved slowly along the shoreline towards her, strong arms bent with the pull of the surf on the line, legs in thigh-high boots planted in a firm stance, shoulders squared, head thrown back against the wind. Slowly, she switched to a telescopic lens and focused on Byron's face in profile. His hair was swept across his forehead, his eyes narrowed, his square jawline set in concentration. He was completely unaware of her. She snapped the shutter. This would be her only personal memory profile, tangible evidence in the long years ahead of a life come close to fulfilment, and he would never know.

He stepped back as a spray of surf splashed against his chest, and she followed his movements, keeping him in focus, snapping the shutter rapidly. Dragging the line through the water, Byron moved slowly closer to her, reeling in, and she kept stepping backwards, following him.

Suddenly she felt the loose rock beneath her feet begin to shift. She flung out her arm for balance, lost her footing, and heard the camera crash against the rocks as she began to slide. She cried out, and the sound of the tumbling rocks was like an avalanche as she sought to catch herself, her fingers grasping only clumps of straw, her feet scraping across wet rocks and mud.

She came to rest at last against a clump of soft earth, dazed and bruised, and for a moment only trying to shake the roaring out of her ears over the amplified sound of her own gasping breaths. There were huge boulders piled up on either side of her, her feet were ploughed into a mound of rocks that completely immobilised them, and in horror she realised what a close call she had really had.

Then she heard a voice. 'Dawn!' It was hoarse and desperate, and weakly she managed to return, 'I'm here!'

Moments later Byron appeared over the crest, his face white and taut, and he made his way with nimble agility over the broken rocks and rubble towards her, not pausing until he had scooped her into his arms, holding her with a crushing force against his chest. 'Oh, my dear God!' he whispered hoarsely. 'Are you all right? I heard the scream, and I looked up and it was like a nightmare—it was you! It was like . . .' He broke off abruptly, as though regretting the display of emotion and the impulsive words, and Dawn felt the warmth go out

of his embrace and its replacement with a strange
sort of tension as he released her, almost with a
forceful effort.

He turned to the rocks which entrapped her,
prying at them with a hostile savagery, hiding his
face from her and his feelings beneath a harsh
tone. 'What in the name of reason were you
thinking of—up here alone, in the rain——'

She replied, fear and confusion turning abruptly
into a more familiar anger, 'I didn't fall on
purpose!'

Byron stopped, his shoulders sagging, his face
still averted, his hand resting limply on a small,
stubbornly wedged stone. For a long time there
was no sound but his carefully regulated breathing
over the whisper of falling mist, and in that
moment all Dawn wanted was to reach out to him,
to say with her heart what her lips could not, to
share with him the truth they had both discovered.
But she waited for him to speak.

He said at last, softly, 'Forgive me, Dawn.' And
still he did not turn to face her. 'I'm—inflexible
sometimes. Too much so, too much of the time.
And hot-tempered. It's just that you frightened me
in a way I never want to be frightened again ...
when I saw you fall and I knew—I knew then I
was going to lose you, and all I could think of was
that my last words to you had been spoken out of
pride, and not what I really felt ... That I'd never
told you how much I loved you, and needed you.
Never.'

He turned to look at her, his eyes open and
streaked with pain, the rain congealing on his face
and looking strangely like tears. And in Dawn
there was pulsating joy mixed with uncertainty, for
she would not move too quickly lest she be hurt

again. She said, searching his face, 'You knew this morning you would lose me—we said goodbye . . .'

Byron shook his head impatiently. 'Pride. Stubbornness. I must have known even then that I couldn't let you go. I've been here all morning, trying to rationalise it, trying to talk myself out of it, and knowing all along that if I came back to the castle and found you gone I would follow you—to Oban, to New York, to the ends of the earth if need be.' He glanced over her shoulder at the turbulent sea for a moment, and then quickly back to her again, his expression intense and searching. 'I've lived my life too long according to a set pattern . . . established values, unquestioned tradition, unbendable rules. It was only when I saw how much those rules were about to cost me that I realised how worthless they really were. You made me see that in this business with Mann—but oh, how much clearer it became when I saw it was about to cost me the only thing that was ever likely to make my life worthwhile!' He smiled at her tenderly. 'You.'

Her eyes were shining, but still she moved cautiously. 'Not all your values and traditions are worthless, Byron . . . you simply carry a good thing too far, sometimes.'

He touched her cheek with a muddy hand, a teasing, affectionate gleam sparking in his eyes. 'Then I'll need you around to keep me in line, won't I?'

Dawn's heart was doing somersaults, her brain bursting with unspoken declarations of ecstasy and love, but she forced herself to say primly, tightening her lips on a smile of pure joy, 'I want to make certain this time. Is that a proposal?'

Byron laughed, an exuberant, unrestrained

sound, and tossed his head back to the wind.
'Dawn, you wretched, impossible little vixen! You
torment me, you set my senses on fire, you make
me angry and you make me helpless in your power
... But I love you, and I can't live without you!'
He controlled his tone into seriousness, and looked
at her. 'Dawn Morrison, my only love, will you
marry me?'

The joy broke though. 'Byron . . .'

He caught the arms which might have gone about
his neck, and his stern tone did not mask the
softening smile that crept across his features. 'No
time for that now, or I'll end up consummating
our agreement here in the mud and rain . . .'
Lightly, his fingers brushed across her cheek to
remove a strand of her hair, and then he
purposefully bent to fling aside the remaining
rocks which trapped her legs. 'But,' he continued,
glancing up once over his shoulder, 'if you can
wait another two weeks for a proper ceremony, I
can promise you a much more comfortable
arrangement ... You're lucky, this boulder took
most of the weight of the rock slide ... Do you
think you can stand?'

He slipped his arm around her waist as he
tossed aside the final rock, and she whispered,
'Yes.'

He smiled. 'Is that in answer to my first
question, or the last?'

'Both,' she answered shyly, and took hold of his
strong arms as he pulled her to her feet.

Then, as they began their slow and cautious
descent, Dawn spied her camera lying crushed
against the rocks, and she could not prevent a cry
of dismay. 'Oh, my camera!'

He laughed a little in tolerant exasperation.

'Ever the professional, my little Rapunzel! Don't worry,' he promised, 'I'll buy you a new one.'

And, on the beach, his supporting arm tight about her, he turned to her, very serious, and once again brushed a strand of hair away from her face. 'For ever,' he said.

She smiled a little timorously and made no response, for everything she had ever needed was in his eyes.

The promise of love.

Harlequin® Plus

A WORD ABOUT THE AUTHOR

Rebecca Flanders is a professional romance author with the ability to write love stories to suit all sorts of different tastes. Not only is she capable of creating novels for Harlequin Presents—*Morning Song* (#632) and *Falkone's Promise* (#666)—but she has already gained recognition as a Harlequin American Romance author. Her novels in that series include *Twice in a Lifetime* (free with subscription), *A Matter of Trust* (#6), *Best of Friends* (#24) and *Suddenly Love* (#41).

Such success, however, was not something that Rebecca achieved overnight. Although she completed her first novel when she was nineteen, it never reached publication — nor did dozens of other attempts during the next few years. Yet these were valuable years for, as the author states, "I spent every spare moment perfecting my skills...until I sold my first novel in 1979."

She was born and raised in the state of Georgia, where she currently lives. She enjoys oil and water-color painting, music—listening and composing—but, she says, with writing and her eleven-year-old daughter keeping her busy, "who has time for hobbies?"

Yours FREE, with a home subscription to
SUPERROMANCE™

Complete and mail
the coupon below today!

- -

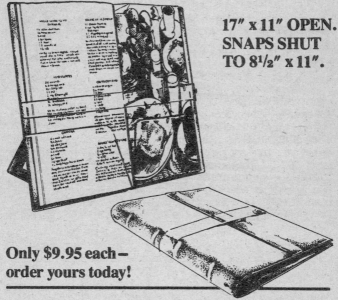

Get this book FREE!

Mail to:

Harlequin Reader Service

In the U.S.
2504 West Southern Avenue
Tempe, AZ 85282

In Canada
649 Ontario Street
Stratford, Ontario N5A 6W2

YES! I want to be one of the first to discover **Harlequin American Romance.** Send me FREE and without obligation *Twice in a Lifetime.* If you do not hear from me after I have examined my FREE book, please send me the 4 new **Harlequin American Romances** each month as soon as they come off the presses. I understand that I will be billed only $2.25 for each book (total $9.00). There are no shipping or handling charges. There is no minimum number of books that I have to purchase. In fact, I may cancel this arrangement at any time. *Twice in a Lifetime* is mine to keep as a FREE gift, even if I do not buy any additional books.

Name _____ (please print)

Address _____ Apt. no. _____

City _____ State/Prov. _____ Zip/Postal Code _____

Signature (If under 18, parent or guardian must sign.) _____

This offer is limited to one order per household and not valid to current Harlequin American Romance subscribers. We reserve the right to exercise discretion in granting membership. If price changes are necessary, you will be notified.

Offer expires August 31, 1984

154 BPA NAP5

AR-SUB-200